# Agape Poppy Book 1: Camping for Christmas

*Dedicated to Jesus Christ*

## Author's Note

Welcome to Agape Poppy Campground Adventures! This book, Camping for Christmas, kicked off the series when it was written in place of a live Christmas play. Agape is widely defined as unconditional love. This is the kind of love God, our "Poppy," has for us. If there is one thing I hope every reader takes away from the story, it is that God loves you unconditionally.

Happy reading!
Madalyn

## **Prologue**

*December 3, 2009*

Mildred O'Dell got up and began looking around her apartment for something made of tin. Just like the tin man in Mr. Baum's story, her granddaughter needed a heart.

Twenty minutes passed, and still no suitable tin item could be found. She really didn't have many belongings anymore. Years of regifting had seen to that.

Mildred went down to the lobby of her building to continue her search.

"Excuse me," she tapped one of the workers.

"Yes, Mrs. O'Dell?" They all knew Mildred very well. She was a staff favorite.

"Could you tell me where I might find a gift made of tin for my granddaughter? She needs a new heart."

The nurse expected a funny request. However, she wasn't expecting to be able to fill it so easily.

"As a matter of fact," the nurse lit up, "there's an artist selling tin stars at the craft fair down the street. They're meant to be tree toppers. Would you like one?"

"That will be perfect," Mildred's eyes were twinkling. She could already tell this was the perfect gift for Emily.

Earlier that day, Mildred picked up the phone. Her wrinkled fingers reached for the number buttons, then fell back down to her side. She ought to know by now that she wouldn't be able to recall any phone numbers. She shuffled over to her address book and glanced at the first page. She kept all of her most used numbers on the first page.

With a hint of frustration at her own aging body, she realized she couldn't see the delicate writing on the worn page without her glasses.

She straightened up and headed for the bedroom.

"Surely those glasses are on my night stand," she thought.

Just as she reached the doorway, the phone rang.

"Please be Charlene," she prayed. If her daughter in law was calling, then she wouldn't need to find the glasses at all.

"Hello?" Mildred greeted the unidentified caller.

"They've been fighting again," Charlene cried on the other end of the line.

"Thank you, Jesus!" Mildred replied, thrilled that she was speaking to Charlene without having had to go through all of the monotonous details of finding the correct telephone number.

"What?" Charlene thought that was an odd response. Maybe Mildred really is *getting old.*

"Oh, nothing," Mildred assured her. "The girls have been fighting?"

"Yes!" Charlene continued, "Emily won't leave Odette alone. She thinks Odette should be doing something all the time. She doesn't understand the need for rest. I wish she'd stop trying to control everyone."

"Did you tell her the story of the prodigal son?" Mildred wondered. That was one of her favorite bible stories.

"Of course not, Emily is hardly going wayward. Odette might benefit, though."

"There's more than one meaning to be gleaned, you know," Mildred was excited to begin lecturing. She hoped Charlene would listen.

"I thought the meaning was perfectly clear," Charlene protested.

"I've always admired how the father didn't try to control the son." Mildred replied. "Love is so free of control, don't you think?"

"Hardly," Charlene muttered. "Mildred, I've got to go soon. Are you comfortable? I was just calling to make sure you're okay."

"No, I'm very *uncomfortable*," Mildred informed her.

"What's the problem?" Charlene wondered.

"I have no idea what to get Emily for her Merry Birthday present."

"I guess a new heart," Charlene replied dramatically. "It'd be great if she softened up some and went easier on Odette. I'll call you back if I think of any tangible ideas."

"I think Mr. Baum has given me an idea or two," it amazed Mildred that she could recall literary heroes but not a telephone number.

"Who?" Charlene wondered if that was one of Mildred's neighbors at the senior center.

"He wrote the Wizard of Oz." Mildred told her triumphantly.

"So not a neighbor, then?" Charlene confirmed.

"I suppose he was somebody's neighbor," Mildred joked.

"Haha. Talk to you later."

"Love you," Mildred smiled through the receiver.

"Love you too."

# Chapter 1

*December 26, 2019*

Emily carefully wrapped the last Christmas decoration and placed it in her suitcase. It was a star tree topper that was her grandmother's eighteenth birthday gift to her. Emily was blessed with a December birthday, so all of her Christmas and birthday gifts were bundled. The careful wrapping of the heirloom probably wasn't necessary. The star was made of punched tin and didn't have anything on it that could fall off.

The wrapping was mostly to protect the gift tag. It read, "God will guide you." Grandma Mildred always made a religious reference on her gifts. Nine years after being tied to the star, the gift tag was still happily attached. It even picked up additional fun memories along the way. On Emily's fourth Christmas with the star topper, her daughter, Rylan, was a lively eight month old baby with pureed sweet potatoes on her soft, chubby fingers. Rylan's precious sweet potato covered thumbprint now lived right under the word "guide" on the gift tag. Emily loved to look at the thumbprint and remember Rylan playing in the bright orange food. When the incident first happened, Emily was upset. That was the last gift she'd received from her grandmother before she passed away. But before she could get too upset, Emily remembered how easy going Grandma Mildred always was about spills. When Emily broke one of Mildred's porcelain dolls, the grandmother's only response was, "my only treasure is your smile," and she gave Emily an extra piece of chocolate. It was Emily's goal to become as easy going as Mildred was.

With her packing complete, Emily's sloppily manicured fingers zipped the suitcase shut, and she thought about how sad she was to be going home. She gazed at her nails. The red and green paint was applied on and off the nail, some places covered, and some not. Despite the uneven coverage, Emily had never seen such a beautiful paint job. Her now six year old daughter wanted to play beauty shop last night. Emily was enthusiastically welcomed to "Rylan's Christmas vacation luxury spa" and promptly received a good hair brushing with watermelon detangling spray and a sparkly pink hairbrush. Once Emily's light blonde hair was satisfactorily brushed, her dedicated spa attendant gave her a hand massage with candy cane lotion and informed her that she would be receiving red and green nails, as was appropriate for the season. It had been the highlight of their trip.

Each year, Emily and Rylan take a special mother-daughter Christmas trip to the same resort and follow, almost, the same routine. This tradition was born out of necessity after Emily's mother, Charlene, got remarried following the death of Emily's father. Charlene kept in touch, but definitely wasn't the present mother Emily had growing up. Emily tried to be understanding, but she couldn't keep her heart from hurting every time Charlene chose to visit with her new step children instead of her. In an attempt to avoid hurt feelings over the holidays, Emily decided to take Rylan out of town so that Charlene wouldn't be able to disappoint them. At the resort, Rylan and Emily watch "Rudolph the Red Nosed Reindeer" the first night, indulging in hot chocolate and popcorn. The next night, they put up the Christmas tree and top it with Grandma's special star. Night three gets silly with board games played by made rules, but night four is the best because it is gift opening time. Emily always loves to watch Rylan open her Christmas presents. She spends hours picking out the "perfect" items. This year, she got Rylan a portable microphone that plays ten different melodies and can record the singer performing. Emily couldn't wait to hear all the little songs Rylan would come up with. She has a beautiful voice.

When they got back home, Emily would return to work and Rylan would go back to school. Their busy schedules would take over and they would have only fleeting moments to be truly together.

Emily heard Rylan singing from the other room.

*Boom boom skat*
*You're a fluffy cat*
*You're whiskers look like Santa's*
*And you're getting kind of fat*
*Boom boom skip*
*Boom boom hop*
*This is how we do the Christmas Trot!*

"Rylan, you better not be singing about me!" Emily called out to her jokingly. Emily might have a whisker or two if she didn't pluck regularly, but she didn't think she looked like Santa or a fluffy cat.

"Of course not!" Rylan replied, "if it was you, I'd be singing about burned popcorn and boxes of tissues."
It was true. Emily burned their popcorn on movie night and went through an entire box of tissues watching "Rudolph."

"Then who are you singing about?" Emily asked.

"This stray kitty! Can we take it home?" Rylan pleaded.

"You know I'm allergic to everything!" Emily called back. Rylan was always begging for a cat.

It was day five and that meant it was time to go. The car would arrive any minute to take the girls to the airport. Emily did a quick check of the suite to make sure they had everything. She tried not to think about all the chores she'd have to do when she got home, but her mind was already scrubbing the floors and washing the sheets of their two bed, one bath condo in the heart of Cedartown, Tennessee.

Emily kept a tidy house, but that wasn't the reason for her

thoughts of cleaning. To pay for their annual trip, she always rented out their condo while they were away. It didn't cover the whole cost, but it certainly helped. The renters usually left the condo in decent shape, but it was still a lot of work to completely disinfect after others have lived in your home for five days.

Emily's attention snapped back to the present as the car arrived.

"Rylan, time to go!" She urged.

"Bye, kitty!" Rylan waved.

"Mom?" Rylan said once they were seated in the back of the car.

"Hmm?" Emily replied as she continued reading her emails. Apparently, work did not stop even though she was on vacation. There might have been some interesting "Front Porch Fall Decor" ideas on her Pinterest board pulling her attention away, too, but only the browse history can confirm that.

"Do you think Francis will still be there next year?" Rylan asked.

Suddenly more aware, Emily asked "Who's Francis?"

"The kitty!" Rylan replied, exasperated. "She was a great listener. I think she really liked my songs."

Emily hadn't realized Rylan spent so much time with the stray cat. Careful to choose her words, she assured Rylan that the kitty would probably still be there, unless she found an even better home.

"An opera singer might adopt her, since she is such a great listener." Emily mused.

"I hope not, Francis really prefers Elvis. Opera might hurt her ears."

Amused, Emily thought about the little tabby flicking its tail along to "Santa Bring My Baby Back To Me" and found herself hoping the cat would still be around next time.

At the airport, there was a wind of officiality in the air.

"Rylan, you'd better hold my hand," Emily encouraged the innocent six year old. They were in line to check their bags.

"Next," a happy young man called to them.

Emily was relieved they seemed to be getting a pleasant attendant to assist them.

"Please place your suitcase on the scale, Miss O'Dell," he instructed her.

Emily lifted the bag onto the scale without worry, it should weigh exactly the same as it did on the way there: 49.8 pounds.

To Emily's horror, a red "50.2" began blinking at her once the bag had been weighed by the electronic tattle tale. Emily had never felt so betrayed by an inanimate object. This scale must be newer and more sensitive than the ones used on the flight out of Cedartown.

"I'm so sorry, Miss O'Dell," the attendant looked genuinely apologetic, "the weight limit is a firm 50 pounds. The computer won't let me print your baggage label until the extra weight is gone. Perhaps you have room to redistribute in your other suitcase?"

"I'm afraid the other suitcase is also near the 50 pound mark," Emily sighed. Maybe she could carry on something like a pair of shoes.

Embarrassed, Emily opened her suitcase, prayed no undergarments were visible, and extracted a pair of dark brown boots.

The attendant happily informed her that the weight was now acceptable and completed the check in process. Now they just had to get through security.

Emily placed her carry on items on the belt to be x-rayed, then got in line behind Rylan to go through the metal detector.

On the other side of the detector, the security officer gave Emily a raised eyebrow.

"There appears to be a Metal Star wrapped up in your boot." The officer informed Emily.

Oops. Emily forgot the star was wrapped up in that particular pair.

"It's a Christmas decoration," Emily explained. "It wouldn't fit in the suitcase."

Another officer came over to examine the suspicious object.

"This is a little too weapon like," she frowned at the five sharp metal points.

"Please, let me put it back in my suitcase then," Emily pleaded.

"That is Grandma's special star," Rylan added.

The security officer shook her head. "It is too late to access your baggage, now. I can have it mailed though, since it is special."

Emily was both annoyed and grateful. She filled out the paperwork and paid the postage fee.

The postal worker that came to collect the star gasped when they saw it.

"It's a real Chip Rangley piece!"

Emily had never heard of Chip Rangley.

"Who's that?"

The worker looked at her in disbelief.
"Chip Rangley is a famous artist who makes sculptures out of trash. He donates most of his proceeds to ocean clean up projects. He got started by making stars like these out of tin cans. Look at the back here," the worker pointed to an inscription etched into the tin material of Emily's star.

It read "C.R."

"This is probably worth at least $500," the worker said. "You'll have to fill out some more paperwork and pay for the insurance before we can mail this."

"Great." Emily wasn't sure how to feel about the newfound value of her special star.

"Glad we didn't throw it away." The security officer quipped.

# Chapter 2

*November 25, 2020*

"Ouch!" Emily cried out as one of her papers cut her finger. She was losing papers left and right trying to answer her ever ringing phone.

"Hello?" She breathed as she answered the call on its last ring.

"Good morning, ma'am!" An overly cheerful male voice boomed over the line.

"Is it?" Emily muttered.

The man continued, "This call is to inform you that your upcoming stay at the Christmas Village Resort and Spa has been cancelled due to COVID restrictions. We hope you understand and stay safe at home!"

"No!" Emily protested, "Our stay can't be cancelled. I've already scheduled for someone to rent out my house for that week. I have nowhere else to go."

Unphased, the man said, "Well ma'am, I suggest you call a relative; all of the hotels are closed under the same restrictions."

He was clearly ready to be done with this conversation. However, Emily wasn't going to give up so easily.

"I don't have anyone, is there really no way to get a room?" She pressed.

Openly agitated now, the man quipped, "Maybe you should try camping. The weather isn't too chilly yet, just pack thermals."

Emily was taken aback.

*Camping!*

"I haven't camped in years," she started.

But the man cut her off, "Should bring up some fun memories then. Have a good day!"

The line went dead.

"Why not?" Emily decided it was better than nothing. She was going camping.

Emily hoped Rylan would be okay with the change. She also hoped her tent was still in storage. She was not in the mood to go tent shopping. She was also not in the mood to think about the painful truth that she didn't have anyone to stay with. The holidays have a way of making you feel bitter when you don't have anyone.

For a moment, Emily thought about texting her mom. It was possible that Charlene had a spare room. It might even be fun to spend time with some of her new relatives. But then she thought about how painful it would be to be a stranger in her own house. The same house where she lost her first tooth and drew a lipstick heart on the wall is now the home to a Mr. and Mrs. Sanders. Emily wasn't even sure that her mom, Charlene O'Dell, was the same woman as Mrs. Charlene Sanders. She pushed the thought aside and tried to focus on the task at hand.

Emily finished putting her work papers in order. There were copies of receipts from business meetings, bank statements and handwritten notes. She had to reconcile all of the information in preparation for the annual audit of her workplace, Caring for Kids Foundation, a nonprofit dedicated to providing healthcare resources for all of Tennessee's children. This would be her first time doing audit prep from home. The COVID-19 pandemic forced her boss, Janet, to close the offices. Emily had a feeling that many of the papers she was currently toting to her car would end up with purple crayon marks permanently etched onto their surface. Rylan is a wonderful, responsible seven year old now, but she couldn't resist adding a bit of purple flare to any paper-based surface.

Emily made it to the front door of the office building when she decided she'd better grab one more thing from her desk. She didn't know how long it might be before she was back in this building. They were living in "unprecedented times," afterall.

Her worn, black tennis shoes turned back and ran up the stairs to her desk. She thought how strange it was to be in the building alone, able to literally run around and sport athletic wear instead of the usual business casual attire.

She didn't even bother flicking the light back on, she knew exactly where the item she was searching for was located. She reached across her keyboard and grabbed a small oval picture frame. It displayed the face of a little baby with huge brown eyes, light brown skin, small black curls and a gorgeous two-toothed smile. It was the picture Emily took of Rylan on May 5th, 2013, her first birthday. On the days when Emily was ready to quit work, the sparkling brown baby eyes reminded her what she was working for.

With papers and motivation in tow, Emily walked back to her car. Rylan was patiently sitting in the backseat working on a detailed drawing of a purple dress.

"Back so soon?" Rylan seemed disappointed.

"I was only grabbing some papers," Emily reminded her.

"But I can't work on my picture if the car is moving, you might hit a bump and make me mess up," The little girl protested.

"I'll turn on some Christmas music and drive really carefully," Emily promised. "What kind of dress is it?"

"It's what Francis wants to wear to the Elvis concert when we see her next month."

"The cat from the resort told you what she wants to wear to an Elvis concert?" Emily was impressed with Rylan's commitment to her ideas, but also heartbroken. She was going to have to tell Rylan that there would be no resort this year, and, consequently, no stray resort cat to play with.

"Of course she did!" Rylan exclaimed. "She hasn't been dressed up in 100 years and can't wait to try on my design. Will you help me make it, Mom?"

"Rylan, you know how everything is closed because of the sickness?"

Rylan gave Emily a hesitant and drawn out "yeeeeeeees."

Emily continued, "The resort is closed just like everything around here. We'll have to go camping instead. But we can mail a dress and a Christmas card to Francis. Will that be okay?"

There was silence from the backseat.

"Rylan?"

"Hold on, Mom, I've got to adjust the dress design into something easier for Francis to put on by herself. I don't think she'll be able to do the buttons without my help. Can cats pull a zipper?"

"Oh, yes." Emily was relieved that Rylan was adjusting so well. She wished she had that kind of resiliency.

"Hey!" Rylan suddenly scolded her.

"What's wrong?"

"You hit a bump."

"Sorry!" It was hard to avoid a little bit of jostling when the streets were covered in speed bumps. Emily genuinely hoped Rylan's picture hadn't suffered too much.

After they got settled at home, Emily began her search for campsites.

*Somewhere warm would be nice*, she thought.

It looked like there were several good options in Florida. One park south of the keys looked particularly inviting.

*Oh, but expensive!* Emily quickly weighed the balance of credit card debt against the amount of joy they were sure to have on the tropical getaway.

She thought it just might be worth the extra dollars. She clicked the "book" button on the campsite screen.

A "Not available" pop up flashed at her brightly.

After an hour of searching for more warm weather campgrounds, Emily was greeted with many more "not available" pop ups.

She never knew how popular it is to go camping for Christmas.

Emily decided to try a campsite closer to home. Tennessee certainly isn't a tropical climate, but it isn't unbearably cold. She would just pray for no snow.

"Agape Poppy Campground and RV Park," that sounds interesting, Emily said to herself. She clicked the cartoon image of an eagle roasting a marshmallow over a campfire.

A clunky website opened with details about primitive and RV camping. Emily clicked the "book now" button without much hope. She thought even this place would be at capacity.

To her surprise, a green calendar appeared with the exact dates she needed marked available.

"Finally!" Emily really was going camping for Christmas. She quickly made the reservation before the miracle disappeared.

# Chapter 3

*November 26, 2020 Thanksgiving Day*

Cheese on the floor. Cheese on the ceiling. Cheese in her hair. Cheese under her nails. Emily didn't even like cheese that much. Sadly, all of the thanksgiving recipes called for cheese, cheese, cheese.

Rylan agreed that the meal was delicious, but she didn't agree that they should clean up and take a nap.

"Shouldn't we hurry up and make the dress for Francis? She's probably anxious to try it on." Rylan nagged her tired mother.

To make the dress, they'd have to go to the storage unit. Emily was going to use some of Rylan's old baby clothes to make the cat outfit. In addition to digging out the baby clothes, she had to find the old family tent.

"I guess we can go ahead and go," Emily gave in to the persistent little girl.

Once they got to the storage unit, Rylan started going through all of her old dresses to find the perfect ones. She found one with lots of glitter and one with lots of ruffles.

"These are perfect!" She exclaimed.

Emily wished she was as enthusiastic about her camping finds. All she felt was sadness at the memories around her. A little bit of bitterness, too.

She tried to ignore those unpleasant feelings and focus on the joy coming out of Rylan.

"I think you're right, my fashion queen!" Emily smiled at her. Those outfits would be easy to work with.

They took their loot back home and got to work. Emily learned a few years ago that she was no good at operating a sewing machine, so there was some very interesting hand stitching with bright purple thread visible on the final product. It was a good thing the dresses Rylan picked out were so cute to begin with. Not even a cheese stain from the disastrous kitchen could make this outfit look bad.

"Are you done yet?" Rylan bounced on her toes next to the table as Emily finished tying one last knot in her thread.

"No, I think I'll start all over. Francis sent me a message saying she doesn't like purple anymore and wants a green dress instead." Emily informed Rylan with a serious expression.

"What! Why would she message you and not me? That isn't right. There must be an imposer!" Rylan stomped her foot and crossed her arms.

"An imposter?" Emily raised her eyebrows. "That would be a very serious problem. Good thing I was only joking about the message. I'm done."

Emily smiled and handed the dress to Rylan.

"Mom! You shouldn't joke like that. I almost called the police!" But despite her scolding, Rylan accepted the dress and tried it on one of her stuffed animals to make sure it would fit the cat.

It fit!

"Great work, Mom," Rylan complimented Emily. "Maybe the queen will call you next time she needs a dress."

"She'll have to call you first," Emily replied. "You are the master designer."

Emily was a little surprised at how well the project turned out. She wasn't exactly a seamstress. None of the women in her family sewed. Actually, no one in her family was very crafty at all. Emily gave herself an invisible high five for getting out of her comfort zone and making the dress with Rylan. She figured that even if it turned out awful, Rylan would probably find a silver lining in it. She has a special gift for finding the silver linings.

Emily helped Rylan write out the address on the box containing the fancy dress. Emily had no idea who would receive the package, but she hoped they thought it was cute.

They addressed it to Francis the Cat at 100 Christmas Village Resort and made sure not to put a return address. Emily didn't want Rylan to be upset if the package came back.

"Do you think Francis had a good Thanksgiving today?" Rylan wondered as they put the final touches on the package.

"Absolutely!" Emily said, "I bet she shared a meal with lots of different families. People get extra generous around the holidays."

"What does it mean to be generous?" Rylan wondered.

"Usually, it means that you share what you have with someone else just to be nice. You don't expect anything in return." Emily explained as she cleaned up some of the mess surrounding them.

"Have we been generous today?" Rylan asked, clearly taking a fascination with the topic.

Emily started to feel uncomfortable. Generosity is a controversial topic for her. Even if it is Thanksgiving Day.

When Emily was a teenager, she was very generous. In the opinion of most, she was too generous. She worked every weekend, but had nothing to show for it on account of giving it all away.

The final straw happened when she was about twenty years old. She allowed someone to live with her for free after hearing a sob story about how he wanted to be a father to his newborn son and a partner to the child's mother, but just couldn't figure out a way for them all to live together. So, Emily opened up her home without hesitation. She even co-signed for the man to get a new car.

The result was the man bringing a completely different woman into the house who was not the child's mother and the unexpected couple used Emily's resources without thanks for months. Emily also got stuck with the car payment. After that horrible experience, Emily saw most people in need as a big danger sign. She kept her distance from anyone asking for help. Except her daughter, of course.

"We could probably find a way to be more generous," Emily admitted to her young do-gooder.

Emily hoped that she would be able to learn the appropriate balance of generosity in time to teach it to Rylan. She didn't want Rylan to make the same mistakes that she did, but she also didn't want her to grow up to be a Scrooge.

Rylan watched Emily expectantly as she thought about how to be generous.

"Maybe we could send a Thanksgiving card to someone in the hospital." Emily suggested. She thought there were online programs for that.

With all of the COVID closures and restrictions, there wasn't much they could do even if she were in a more generous spirit.

"That sounds like fun!" Rylan liked the idea of another project.

Emily got on the computer and looked up the website for their local hospital. Sure enough, there was a place to upload a hand drawn card if you wanted to share a picture with one of the patients. She and Rylan got to work.

"What should we draw?" Emily asked Rylan after they stared at the blank page for a few seconds.

"The sun?" Rylan suggested. "The sun makes everyone happy."

"Sounds fine to me!" Emily agreed.

The resulting picture wasn't what Emily expected when Rylan said "the sun." It was a picture of several suns, and they were all doing different things.

One sun was sleeping in late. One was eating lots of chocolate. One was taking a bubble bath. And the last one was riding a purple unicorn.

"This should definitely make the patient feel more…sunny," Emily told Rylan and took a photo of the colorful drawing.

Before she uploaded the photo to the hospital website, Emily sent a copy to her mom via text message with the caption "Sunny Days by Rylan."

Her mom immediately replied, "Precious! Love it."

Emily felt encouraged by the quick response and asked if she could call later. She soon wished she hadn't.

Charlene texted, "can't talk until late. Lots of people are over."

Emily closed the text messages and went back to the hospital website. "Sunny Days by Rylan" was going to be sent to Ms. Mary D. with the note "We hope you like soaking up all of these sun rays!" Emily never knew what to say to people in the hospital, but since it was coming from a seven year old girl, she thought it would be alright.

"Have we been generous now, mom?" Rylan asked when Emily finished sending the card.

"I think we've been as generous as we can today," Emily said. "If you want to be more generous, maybe you should make a list of ideas. I'll help you with them tomorrow. Right now I've got to do some work."

"I don't like you working so much at home," Rylan admitted.

"I don't like it either," Emily confessed. "But with the office closed, I have to do all the work here. At least we get to take breaks together."

"That's true. It is just lonely when you have to work."

Emily didn't have a solution for that. School had been closed for months because of COVID. She assumed all of the kids were pretty lonely. It wasn't advised to have play dates, either. You never knew who had been exposed to what.

"I'll only work for one hour and then we'll watch something together. Deal?"

"Deal! Hey mom?"

"Yes?" Emily reflected on how difficult it is to work from home with so many distractions.

"Can we make another card later? I want to draw us camping."

# Chapter 4

*December 19th, 2020 Emily's Birthday*

*Don't think about it,* Emily warned herself. She already spent the whole night thinking about it. Now the cycle of dread was rolling into her morning.

Scenes from movies and tv shows played in her mind on an unwelcome loop. Scenes of happy families celebrating birthdays and holidays. Scenes that did not mirror her own recent experience. There is a deep root of bitterness planted in her heart. A root that she has no idea how to get out. She wished she could just be content with whatever happened on her "special day," but she already knew that nothing would make her happy.

As expected, Emily received a text message from her mom at exactly 12:00 AM reading: *Happy birthday, Emily! You are so special. I'm very proud of the woman you've become. You are an amazing mother to Rylan and an inspiration to me. I love you!*

Emily thought about not saying anything in reply, but instead she gave the appropriate response: Thanks so much! Love you too.

She then tossed her phone aside and decided to make herself a celebratory birthday breakfast. Maybe if she went through the motions of celebrating she would feel more joyous.

The scene she came upon when she left her bedroom was certainly more than she expected.

There were sticky notes all over the house. They were in the hallway, on the couch, in the fridge, and even in the bathroom.

Each note had a crayon drawing proudly displayed on its surface. Emily got to enjoy pictures of balloons, cakes, puppies, kitties, happy faces, silly faces, flowers, snow men, fireworks, princesses, butterflies, campfires, tents, trees, and more.

Rylan really outdid herself this year.

Emily peeked into Rylan's room, she was asleep on the floor with crayons around her.

The outpouring of love was more than Emily could handle. She went back to her own room and cried. She wasn't sure if she was more happy or more sad. She was simply emotional.

Her heart felt much more vulnerable after seeing the physical representation of how much her daughter loved her. Emily wasn't sure if Rylan would even remember her birthday. Emily did mention it the day before just to see if it would matter, but she didn't think it would stick.

Yet, stick it did.

While she waited for Rylan to wake up, Emily made herself some birthday bacon and drank a glass of chocolate milk while she scrolled through her emails. She was still trying to find a miracle budget solution for work. One of the things she noticed while reconciling all of the budget numbers was that the expense column was becoming increasingly larger than the revenue column.

Instead of the miracle budget solution she was hoping for, Emily was surprised to see an email message from Pamela A. Brooks, Manager of Agape Poppy Campground and RV Park.

*Emily,*

*The Agape Poppy Team is so happy you've decided to join us for the Christmas season!*

*You can check in to your campsite on December 22nd anytime between sunrise and sunset. For your safety, check ins will not be permitted after dark.*

*A map of the campground is attached for your convenience along with a list of typical essentials needed to enjoy a comfortable stay.*

*As part of our effort to spread joy this season, we are requesting that all guests bring one canned item to donate to our local food bank. Cans will be collected at the check in desk.*

*Please reach out if you have any questions. We look forward to seeing you soon!*

*Many thanks,*
*Pamela A. Brooks*
*Manager*
*Agape Poppy Campground and RV Park*

Emily saved a copy of the packing list and made a mental note to bring a can for the food drive. She thought it was interesting that a campground was collecting food for charity. She never thought much before about the various ways a campground could get involved in programs. Maybe there is an opportunity for her workplace to partner with Agape Poppy on a project.

*There won't be opportunity for anything if the budget isn't fixed,* Emily reminded herself.

Just as she began to fall into the mental hole of finding new revenue streams, Emily felt a small force tackling her to the floor.

With Rylan gleefully laying on her face, Emily got to listen to the extended version of "Happy Birthday, Mommy!"

By the time the song was over, the pain from hitting the floor had abated.

"Didn't you like your song?" Rylan asked the birthday girl while still sitting on her head.

Emily replied with muffled noises.

"Oh!" It finally occurred to Rylan that Emily wasn't talented enough to say thank you with her mouth covered. She stood up and asked again.

"Did you like it?"

Emily gave Rylan a big hug. "I loved it. I love the decorations, too."

"Are we going to get cake for breakfast?" Rylan asked hopefully.

"I thought we could save the cake for later," Emily admitted. "Maybe we could invite some of your dolls to come to the kitchen for a birthday tea party?"

Rylan loved that idea. Tea parties were her favorite.

"Will we get to wear dresses?" Rylan wondered.

"It is required!" Emily used her best British accent, "One must look their best to properly enjoy tea."

"I guess I'll have to be careful which dolls I invite," Rylan mused. Some of her toys could be a little messy. That simply wouldn't do for the civilized tea party.

"I only have enough cake for three dolls," Emily advised.

"I'll start the interviews now!" Rylan excitedly ran to her room to decide which three dolls would be attending the auspicious occasion.

Emily sat some breakfast items out for Rylan in case she remembered to eat between interviews.

With Rylan occupied, Emily decided she had to do something to work on the budget problem. She started submitting grant applications on every funding site she could find. Some of the applications were definitely a stretch, but nothing ventured, nothing gained.

Rylan emerged from interviewing her dolls several times to eat some fruit and oatmeal bars out of the kitchen.

"Mom?"

Emily raised an eyebrow at the all too familiar sound of being needed.

"Are you ready to pick who is coming to the party?" Rylan asked. "I've narrowed the list down to five."

"Five?" Emily pretended to be horrified, "That will never do. We must have only three. Bring in these party crashers."

Rylan excitedly lined up five of her favorite dolls. Emily noticed they were all dressed in their best ball gowns. She was glad to see that Rylan is taking the tea party seriously.

"Who is my first victim?" Emily surveyed the line up.

"First is Alice Ann," Rylan presented a doll wearing a pink dress and a tangle of blonde hair that tumbled past her hips.

"How do you do, Alice," Emily greeted the doll.

"Alice Ann," Rylan reminded her.

"Excuse me," Emily corrected herself. "How do you do, Alice Ann?"

"Nervous," Alice Ann admitted in a voice that sounded suspiciously like Rylan's.

"I appreciate your honesty, Alice Ann. That will take you far in life," Emily encouraged the doll.

"So I can come to the party?" Alice Ann was jumping ahead of herself.

"Slow down!" Emily frowned and pretended to make notes. "You haven't told me what you would be bringing to the party."

"I'm very good at cooking pies," Alice Ann said brightly.

"That's nice for you," Emily replied, "but I already have a cake. I don't need a pie. Maybe you can come to Thanksgiving Tea next year. Next!"

"Alice Ann! I told you not to talk about pie," Rylan scolded the doll.

The next potential guest was a doll wearing a glittery white gown and a tiara. She had a very classy brunette updo, too.

"Hello, Miss..?" Emily reached out to shake the doll's hand.

"Holly," The classy brunette replied. She also sounded a bit like Rylan.

"Well, Holly, what would you bring to the tea party?" Emily inquired.

"Towels!" Holly declared.

"In case of spills?" Emily wondered.

"I never spill," Holly explained, "but I saw you don't have any clean towels. So I thought you might like some."

"That's very thoughtful, Holly. One point for you!" Emily liked almost everything about Holly. There was just one thing wrong…

"Holly?"

"Yes?"

"I see you're wearing a tiara." Emily noticed.

"It is part of my head," Holly said apologetically.

"That is most unfortunate," Emily sympathized with her. It must be dreadful not to be able to at least put on a new tiara once in a while. "The problem is that today is my birthday, so I am the only one allowed to wear a tiara."

"I cover it up with hats all the time!" Holly insisted.

"Perfect!" Emily was thrilled that Holly would be an acceptable birthday guest. "You may arrive at the birthday tea at exactly 4:30

PM."

"Thank you!" Holly gave Emily a big hug. Rylan proceeded to voice the next three dolls.

Emily interviewed a Belle, a Lottie, and an Emily. She wanted Lottie to come, but it seems that Lottie came down with a cold in the middle of the interview, so she got stuck with Belle and the other Emily.

When Emily expressed her displeasure to Rylan at having another Emily at her birthday tea, Rylan simply shrugged and said, "Life be like that."

# Chapter 5

*December 21, 2020*

"Is it pirate day?" Emily asked her boss, Janet, when she joined the video call.

Janet was put together as usual, except today she was sporting a black eyepatch.

"There was an incident," Janet explained.

"Oh?" Emily could use a good story. She had spent her morning adding numbers to spreadsheets while listening to a certain ice princess cartoon sing the same song on repeat.

"I tried to put on eyelash enhancers this morning," Janet began. "Bu-"

Emily cut her off, "Do you mean fake eyelashes?"

"I prefer to think of them as enhancers," Janet insisted. "Anyway, they were the wrong kind. There are bright red sparkles on the lash tips. When I tried to pull them off, they just got stuck in between my eyelid and eyebrow. I'll look up how to get it off after the call."

Emily was desperate to see this spectacle, "Couldn't you give me a quick peek?"

Janet pretended to sigh and lifted the eyepatch. After Emily had a good laugh, the eyepatch went back in place and they proceeded to meet about the budget.

Emily advised that they needed to find a new revenue stream.

Maybe more than one. With nonprofits, funding is always tricky.

"I know, but with COVID going on it is almost impossible to get new projects going," Janet had already asked around to see if there were any grants available. She didn't know how they could find a new revenue stream in this pandemic era.

Emily relayed her own searching endeavors. Janet was impressed that Emily had already submitted some applications.

After her call with Janet, Emily was content to research more opportunities, but Rylan had a different idea.

"Mom, what is urine?"

"That is another name for pee. Why do you ask?" Emily didn't enjoy questions about potty words. She never knew where these conversations were going.

"The commercial says we need to spray lots of wolf urine to keep the bears away. If we order it now, will it be here before we leave tomorrow?"

"I don't think so," Emily replied honestly. "But there aren't any bears at this campsite."

"How can you be sure?" Rylan loved most animals, but she knew wild bears were not her friend.

"Well the website didn't say anything about bears," Emily opened the Agape Poppy website up on her laptop and showed Rylan.

They scrolled through pictures of ducklings, deer, hawks, herons, squirrels, beavers, and chipmunks.

"See? There's not a single bear on here," Emily said happily.

"I guess you're right," Rylan admitted. "All of the bears must be at a different camp."

"Must be!" Emily agreed.

"Do you think the people camping around the bears knew to bring wolf pee?" Rylan thought that maybe this wasn't just new information to her.

"Absolutely! Everyone has wolf pee." Emily went back to her spreadsheet and saw an alarming number.

An alarmingly negative number.

Her projections for next year's budget were not going well. If she didn't find a new revenue stream, they would have to let one of the employees go.

"Hey Rylan, did your commercial say anything about internet access in the woods?" Emily had no idea how she'd be able to figure this out before they left for their camping trip.

"No, but I'll keep watching in case that comes up," Rylan gave Emily a thumbs up.

Emily sent Janet an email with the budget information and a few ideas about how to solve the problem. One of the ideas included salary cuts. Emily was filled with anxiety over the issue. She didn't know how she would support herself and Rylan if she had to take a pay cut. She didn't like the idea of finding a different job. She felt that new beginnings were always painful.

*Maybe a miracle will happen.* Emily thought to herself.

Later that evening, Rylan was dancing around her room. Tomorrow, they were going camping for Christmas. It was a dream come true! Rylan had never been camping before, but all the movies made it look fun.

Emily walked in on Rylan singing:

*I'm going to build a snow man,*
*Or maybe just play in mud,*
*I'm going to pet a raccoooooon,*
*Or find buried treasure with my mooooooooommmmm.....*

"Buried treasure? You want me to dig?" Emily pretended to be offended.

"No way, mom!" Rylan offered, "We will get the raccoon to do the digging."

"I didn't know you could train a raccoon to do your dirty work." Emily marveled.

"Who else is going to do it? They are nature's bandits." Rylan stated.

"If they are bandits, won't they steal our treasure?" Emily wondered.

"Uh oh, you're right," Rylan started looking around her room frantically.

"What are you looking for?" Emily walked over to the closet so she could look, too.

Rylan peeked out from under her bed, "A lock! I don't want raccoons stealing my stuff."

"Ah. Are you packed? There won't be anything to steal if you don't get that done," The nagging mom persona was overtaking the silly one.

"Almost," Rylan cheerfully assured her. "I just need to get the star."

"The star?" Emily felt a surge of sadness, "I don't think we can take Grandma's star camping. The tag might get broken and we won't have a tree, anyways."

Rylan was confused, "aren't there lots of trees in the woods?"

Emily smiled, "Yes, but none that I could reach to put a star on top of."

"You are short," Rylan agreed.

"Maybe your raccoon friends can climb to the top for us?" Emily countered.

"No, no, no," Rylan shook her head, dark curls bouncing all around her sweet face, "the raccoon would just steal the star. Remember? They are BANDITS."

"My bad," Emily threw her hands up in mock surrender. She wondered how they were going to fill their days without a tree to decorate, movies to watch, or presents to unwrap. They did gifts a week early so that they wouldn't have to carry them to the campsite.

Emily's alarm went off.

"Why is your phone beeping?" Rylan asked.

"Because it is time to go to bed, we have a big day tomorrow! We have to get to the campsite early so we can get the tent up before dark," Emily explained.

"I didn't know you could set an alarm to make you go to sleep. I thought they were just to wake you up," Rylan didn't like the idea of the alarm bossing her around all day. She hoped it couldn't make her do other things, like clean her room.

"You can set an alarm to remind you about anything," Emily told her.

Great. It was just as Rylan feared, the alarm could get all in her business.

Emily tucked Rylan into bed and sang her special lullaby:

*Twinkle twinkle little Rylan,*
*It makes my heart swell to see you smilin'*
*Laughing here,*
*(Emily gave her a good tickling)*
*Laughing there,*
*A hug and a kiss on your pretty hair,*

*Twinkle twinkle little Rylan,*

*You're more special than all the diamonds*

"Goodnight, sweet heart," Emily whispered and went out to the living room where all of their camping gear was gathered.

The last time Emily went camping was when she was fifteen years old. That was thirteen years ago. Her parents took her and her younger sister, Odette, to a campground near an amusement park. Their family didn't camp often. The trip was brought on by her father's cancer diagnosis. He had a short amount of time left and didn't want to pass without showing his girls how to camp. Emily remembered the trip fondly, but also bitterly. She missed her father. She missed her family. Her mother, Charlene, was remarried and had little time for Emily. No one knew where Odette was. She moved away the week after her high school graduation and didn't leave any contact information.

The tent Emily was able to dig out of storage is the one from that family camping trip. It is big enough for four people and is a faded burgundy color. Emily also found the sleeping bags she and Odette slept in. They have a nice polka dot pattern that Rylan will probably enjoy. Maybe she could bring along some fabric markers and let Rylan color on the tent as one of their activities. Anything would make this tent look better.

Emily ran her hand over the backpack containing the tent and the sleeping bags. She pictured her dad holding her and Odette in his arms while singing "Oh, Susannah," the only "campfire song" he knew.

She allowed herself to cry at the pain of missing those years. But the tears weren't allowed to keep her from her checklist.

Emily made sure they had all of the essentials ready to go. The only thing she had to pack in the morning was the cooler.

Semi-confident that she was prepared for their adventure, Emily went to bed.

Rylan dreamed of raccoons finding gems and jewels around their campsite. Emily dreamed about their tent blowing away and raccoons eating their food.

# Chapter 6

*December 22, 2020*

"Go fish," Nate said to Gabe after Gabe asked if he had any threes.

Nathaniel, "Nate," Boom and Gabriel, "Gabe," Brooks are the full time park rangers at Agape Poppy Campground and RV Park. They are longtime best friends and have most things in common, except appearance. Nate is an average height with short golden hair and slightly slanted blue eyes. His uniform was always tidy and his face stayed clean shaven. Gabe is a giant man, towering over most at six feet five inches, and kept his light brown hair long and shaggy. His beard was always bushy in winter and his deep brown eyes were framed by square black glasses. He inherited more of the Cuban appearance than his mom, Pam, did. His grandmother was one of the many Cuban refugees who arrived to the US in 1959 when Castro came to power.

"You say that about every number!" Gabe accused, but drew a card.

"Hello?" Emily called into the seemingly empty ranger station. She noticed a strong smell of beef jerky.

"Did you know we had another check in today?" Nate asked Gabe.

"Yeah, but I didn't think she'd show!" Gabe was surprised. On the phone, Emily sounded very much so like she did not want to come camping. She even asked if he knew of any hotels that might be open.

"Better put on your mask and your positive attitude," Gabe warned Nate, "this one will be interesting."

The rangers walked out to the front desk.

"Hello, campers!" They said in unison.

Nate began their carefully practiced welcome script: "Welcome to Agape Poppy Campground. You can be sloppy or drive a jalopy, but don't expect an indoor potty."

"Oh, dear." Emily was having second thoughts about this.

"We are your park rangers for the week," Gabe continued, "I'm Ranger Gabriel Brooks."

"And I'm Ranger Nathaniel Boom. We can't wait to show you all the fun to be had out here on God's green earth."

Nate pulled out a map, "Your campsite is just down this path," he pointed at a very narrow line that intermingled with other lines in various places.

Emily stopped him, "Won't you be taking us to our campsite?"

Nate started to answer, but Gabe interrupted, "I'd love to take you to your campsite." Emily might have been difficult on the phone, but she sure was a beauty in person. He was looking forward to spending the week with her.

Nate gave him a confused look, but played along, "I'll go saddle up the horses for you."

"Horses?" Rylan's excitement burst forth at the mention of real animals.

"Horses?" Emily wasn't keen to encounter that much nature so soon into their trip.

"It's the easiest way," Gabe explained, "The park manager doesn't allow motor vehicles on the trails and you seem to have a lot of bags to carry."

"Everyone says she has a lot of baggage," Rylan offered. Emily's face went red.

Gabe stifled a laugh, "Good thing I have strong horses. Let's go meet them."

On their way out the door, Rylan noticed a large painting of a particularly beautiful cat.

"Come on, Rylan," Emily encouraged the dawdling child.

"But Mom, look!" Rylan wasn't eager to leave the cat painting so quickly. Its eyes were hypnotizing.

Gabe looked proud and sad at the notice of the painting. "My dad made that," he explained. "He was a great artist. That is a portrait of the family cat, Chip."

"Is Chip around here somewhere?" Rylan immediately began scanning the room for any trace of a feline. She couldn't resist the opportunity to pet a cat.

"Sadly, no." Gabe shifted uncomfortably. "My dad and Chip both passed away about ten years ago."

Gabe hated having to tell people those dark details. He preferred to keep conversation light, especially on a Christmas camping trip.

He brightened, "But my horses are very much alive. You'll like them."

Rylan and Emily followed Ranger Brooks to the stables. When she saw the horses, Emily was amazed at how friendly they seemed.

"Can I pet him?" Rylan asked Ranger Brooks, pointing at a large, black horse.

"Her, actually." Gabe replied, "That is
Miss Irma. You can pet her and give her a treat." He handed Rylan a sugar cube and showed her how to feed the horse with her hand extended out, palm up, and flat.

The tall ranger turned his dark gaze to Emily, "Do you want to try?" He offered her a sugar cube for Miss Irma.

"I'd better not," Emily backed away, "I'm allergic to horses."

"She's allergic to everything," Rylan confirmed.

"I hope you brought your Benadryl," Ranger Gabe Brooks joked. "If not, I hear wolf pee takes the edge off any allergic reaction."

The rangers were used to new campers thinking wolf urine could fix everything. He wouldn't be surprised if these city dwellers brought some along.

Rylan's eyes grew wide, "I told you we should have ordered some!" She said to Emily.

Emily was not amused, "Don't worry, the rangers here will have it in stock since it is so useful."

Nate returned with four horses ready to ride. The rangers helped the girls get saddled up and then secured a lead rope to their bridles.

Emily was glad the rangers were guiding them to their campsite, she would never have found her way without their help.

The horses trudged over countless puddles and the rangers knocked down at least three spider webs as they made their way to "Campsite number 1."

Emily barely heard Ranger Boom ask Ranger Brooks something in a hushed tone as they led the girls down the path.

"Did Pam figure out the dream?"

Gabe Brooks shook his head no, "I told her to try reading about the wise man and the foolish man."

"That's probably a good place to start," Nate agreed.

"I hope she doesn't have the dream again tonight," Gabe said.

"Same. She gets kind of moody when she doesn't sleep well."

"Isn't this a little far?" Emily interrupted. She didn't feel comfortable being such a great distance from the ranger station.

"Don't worry!" Nate replied, "There is a large group camping next to you at site number 2."

"Plus, we patrol the area frequently," Gabe chimed in.

"It is so pretty out here!" Rylan was admiring all the leaves and pine needles.

"You have a nice view of the lake," Nate pointed out. They were at the campsite now, and Emily wasn't impressed.

"That's it?" She surveyed the empty patch of land next to the water.

"Yeah," Gabe shrugged.

"Don't you like it?" Nate couldn't believe anyone wouldn't like the Agape Lake. It reflected the sky beautifully and there were always plenty of birds around it.

Emily handed her tent to Gabe, "Maybe after you set up the tent it will be more...desirable."

"We usually don't do the set up," Nate began to tell her.

Gabe cut him off again, "But if you say please, then I guess Ranger Boom and I wouldn't mind." He winked.

*Was he flirting with her?* Emily felt a flicker of hope, then gave herself a reality check. She reminded herself that this is not a love story.

"Please," Emily rolled her eyes.

"Pleaaaase! Please, please, please!" Rylan jumped all around the campsite. She was eager to get unpacked.

"Happy to help! It is Christmas time, after all," Gabe smiled. The rangers proceeded to set up camp and tell the girls about local flora and fauna.

Once the rangers were done, Rylan got to feed the horses more sugar cubes and then the men departed.

Emily was looking forward to reading her magazine and having some quiet "me time" after the long day of travel.

"So mom," Rylan peeked over Emily's magazine, "what's for dinner?"

Emily wasn't thrilled at first about the thought of cooking dinner, but then she remembered the luxurious contents of her cooler.

"Well, we can have steak with potatoes, barbecue sandwiches with coleslaw, or teriyaki chicken with carrots." She might have lost her stay at the five star resort, but Emily was not about to lose her resort style dinners. She did not want to live off pinto beans and lake fish for the week. She invested in some top of the line camping equipment, like her extra cool cooler, to be able to have delicious meal options. She even studied the art of spice mixing and pre-seasoned all the food herself.

Rylan chose the teriyaki chicken and Emily got up to dig it out of the cooler.

The cooler.

It was missing.

The rangers must have forgotten to pack it up when they were leaving the station. Emily chided herself for not checking.

"Sorry, Princess, it looks like dinner will be awhile. The cooler is missing."

"Did the raccoons steal it?" Rylan wondered.

"If they did, they'll be hearing from my lawyer," Emily replied. She had no idea how they were going to find food. The sun was setting and she didn't know how to get back to the station.

"Mommy, do raccoons play music?"

"I'm not in the mood to play games, sweetie. I'm trying to figure out what to do about food." Emily was becoming increasingly worried. Camping was a scarier experience than she anticipated.

"I'm not playing!" Rylan insisted, "I hear music!"

Then, Emily heard it, too. There was a banjo playing "It Came Upon a Midnight Clear," and the tune was growing louder. Someone must be coming! Emily's spirits soared. *They would be okay!*

Two young men entered the clearing wearing matching purple sweatshirts. One carried a banjo and the other sang:

*Still thru the cloven skies they come*
*With peaceful wings unfurled,*
*And still their heav'nly music floats*
*O'er all the weary world.*
*Above its sad and lowly plains*
*They bend on hov'ring wing,*
*And ever o'er its babel sounds*
*The blessed angels sing.*

Emily interrupted the musicians, "Excuse me! We need help."

The banjo player gave her a reassuring smile, "Not to worry, miss, we can help you. We're from the church group camping next door."

The singer joined in on the introductions, "We always visit the other campers to sing carols, it is a great way to spread the joy of Jesus."

The banjo player picked back up, "My name is Jamey and this is Kenaniah. What sort of help do you need?"

Emily was trying to be polite but felt so frantic, she wasn't sure if she succeeded, "Our cooler is missing. We don't know how to get food" she stammered.

Jamey suddenly understood why Lilly, their designated camping chef, always packed extra food.

"Would you like to join us for dinner?" Jamey asked.

"We're having hotdogs," Kenaniah added.

"I love hotdogs!" Rylan cheered.

"That sounds wonderful," Emily was so relieved. The girls followed the cheerful musicians down a winding path surrounded by pine trees. Emily wished it were warm enough for fireflies. The soft glow of the little bugs would have made the walk magical. The boys continued their caroling with "Oh Christmas Tree," but it wasn't a version she was familiar with.

*Oh, Christmas Tree,*
*Oh, Christmas Tree,*

*How clearly you remind us*
*The God of Love*
*The Prince of Peace*
*Was born to lead and guide us*

*The angel said, "Don't be afraid!*
*Look, good news to you I bring*
*Your savior has been born today*
*Christ the Lord, forever reign!*

*Oh, Father God,*
*Oh, Holy Ghost,*

*We long for your love the most*

*Oh, Christmas tree,*
*Jesus saved me,*

*Thank you for eternity*

As Jamey strummed the last chord, Emily realized her thoughts had drifted to her childhood and she had not been watching the path. She hoped someone from the church group would lead them back. They were out of sight of the lake.

The trail opened up to a narrow campsite hedged in by the forest on one side and a short waterfall on the other. A large cabin was nestled up a hill by the waterfall, and small tents were pitched around on patches of level ground. Emily couldn't imagine a more quaint setting. Well, actually, she could. The whole scene would look better without the mismatched tents cluttering up the clearing. Nonetheless, it was still beautiful. Emily wished she and Rylan were staying at this location. She loved waterfalls.

"Oh good!" A woman in one of the matching purple sweatshirts came up and waved a chore wheel at the musicians.

"Jamey, Kenaniah, it is y'alls turn to do the dishes tonight. I was starting to think you were skipping out on your chores." The woman handed them aprons and smiled at Emily and Rylan. "Who's this?"

"Bliss, these are our neighbors from campsite 1," Jamey presented the girls to Bliss.

"Emily and Rylan O'Dell," Emily extended her hand to the woman.

"Well it is so nice to have guests!" Bliss ignored the hand and hugged the girls instead, "you ladies just make yourselves at home. I'll get you some sweet tea and hot dogs."

Soon, they were all seated around the fire with the rest of the group. The pastor, a man named Ernest Long, called for everyone's attention to bless the food.

"It feels good to be alive today, amen?" Pastor Long shouted and raised his arms to the heavens. The congregation returned his 'amen' and several clapped.

The man then raised his hand up in a wait signal and walked directly towards Rylan and Emily.

*Please don't make a scene.* Emily silently prayed. She didn't like to be on display.

Pastor Long must have read her mind. He gave Emily a welcoming grin and then extended his hand towards Rylan.

"Young lady," he shouted, " I cannot continue the worshipping of the good lord until I've had a proper handshake. Do you know how to do a proper handshake? The folks around here sometimes struggle with it."

Unlike Emily, Rylan loves to be on display. She is a natural performer and was basking in the unexpected attention.

"I can handshake!" She told the pastor.

"Let's see it then! Keep up as best you can," Pastor Long grabbed her hand, shook it three times, clapped, spun around, hopped, shook her hand again, shook the other hand, turned around again, then touched his toes.

By the time he was done, Rylan and the whole group had a case of the giggles.

"That was some excellent hand shaking!" Pastor Long gave Rylan an encouraging pat on the back. "I'm glad I've found someone who can keep up with me."

He continued, "I praise God, yes, I praise him, for the many blessings he has given us." More 'amens' could be heard throughout the group. Emily was intrigued by the participation. The pastor had not even reached the climax of his sermon, yet so many people seemed to be filled with passion. There was an energy there she had never felt before.

"God created this beautiful earth and allows us to enjoy it," Ernest gestured around them. "Just look at the detail He placed into each element of this clearing. God puts even more love and care into each of us, his children. In Psalm 139, verse 14 King David sings, 'I *will praise thee; for I am fearfully and wonderfully made: marvellous are thy works; and that my soul knoweth right well'."* Pastor Ernest paused to sip some water and wipe his brow. The weather was cold, but his excitement as he preached was making him sweat.

"Preach!" One of the congregants gave an encouraging yell.

"I ask you this, brothers and sisters," each person felt as if the pastor was staring into their souls. "If God made us wonderfully and is taking care of our every need, why are we not celebrating? Our journey ought to be overflowing with joyful worship as we share the good news about Christ. We've got to participate, listen, and persevere."

Ernest must have heard the grumbling of hungry stomachs around him, he wrapped up with, "Ecclesiastes 3 tells us that there is a time for everything. I declare it is now time to enjoy the fruits of our labor as we fellowship with one another over dinner!"

With all heads bowed and eyes closed in reverence, he prayed, "Father God, we come before you in this moment to thank you for what you have done and are doing in our lives. Thank you for this beautiful land, for this delicious food, the hands that made it, and the guests we have received. Lord, we ask you to bless this time. Let your spirit move among us and let all hearts be open. Amen." The congregation gave another resounding 'Amen' and then dug into their meal.

Rylan spent her time around the campfire telling a group of the church ladies how she wanted to decorate her room in the new year.

"Do you change your room every year?" A woman named Sally asked her.

"Not every year, but mom said I can change it this year because I don't like pink anymore. I like purple!"

"My favorite color is green," another of the ladies, Linda, told her.

"Green!" Rylan exclaimed, "I don't want a green room. Do you have a green room?"

"No, but I did paint green vines in my room. I painted in little birds and butterflies, too." Linda replied.

"Oh yes! I would love some purple butterflies in my room," Rylan dreamed of purple butterflies floating all around her bed.

"I bet your stuffed animals would like a little castle to live in," Sally remarked. She loved to decorate.

"A purple castle!" Rylan was enthralled with the idea now. She even owned a "pet dragon" that could guard the castle.

Emily tuned into their conversation, she had been discussing goats with a girl around her age named Emory. Apparently, goats make wonderful pets.

"What's this about a purple castle?" Emily asked the decorating group and Rylan.

"For my stuffies!" Rylan told her, referring to her stuffed animals.

"It would be easy to make one out of cardboard," Sally said, already envisioning how she could make it.

"She could put a purple flower garden around it, too," Linda added. She was a flower expert.

"That sounds pretty," Emily was amazed that the women cared so much about Rylan's room. "Thank you for listening to her and for the ideas."

"Anytime!" Sally gushed.

"We love talking to young people," Linda smiled. "They are just as important as anyone else."

That struck a chord with Emily. She wished there had been kind people like that around her when she was younger. Sometimes, it is difficult to get attention.

From her conversation with Emory, Emily found out that the group was from Shepherd Springs Church in Cedartown. They were located just about fifteen minutes from where Emily and Rylan live. They are a smaller church and several of the people on the camping trip weren't actually church members. Emily thought she had probably seen some of them around town before. She hoped she had been nice to all of them in traffic.

Dinner was simple, but delicious and filling. It was fun to roast their own hot dogs around the fire and to converse with the church members. Emily had no idea what time it was; in her worry over getting Rylan something to eat, she left her phone at her tent. She usually wore a watch, but it broke while she was packing up the car at their condo to go camping. It was oddly freeing not to be controlled by the time or her devices.

"Are you ready to head back to your campsite?" A familiar voice asked her.

It was Ranger Brooks! *How did he get there?*

Gabe must have seen the confusion on Emily's face when she turned around.

"We always patrol all the campsite trails around the clock to make sure everyone is okay. Camping can be dangerous," he explained. "I'm taking first watch while Ranger Boom gets some sleep. I'll show you the way back, if you're ready."

Rylan would have talked to the other campers all night, but Emily could tell they were ready for bed.

"Lead the way," she told Ranger Brooks.

On the way back, Gabe tried to talk to Emily about the stars, but it wasn't going so well.

"Over there is Orion's Belt," he pointed vaguely up and then realized it was too cloudy to see. Embarrassed, he backtracked "I guess it is a little cloudy tonight. You can't really see it."

Emily wanted to change the subject, stargazing was a little too romantic for her taste.

"Good thing it wasn't cloudy the night Jesus was born!" She joked.

Surprised, Gabe answered, "Yeah, that might have made things difficult for the wise men. God really knows what he's doing."

This was the first time Emily indicated she might be religious. It made Gabe feel more hopeful. He would much rather discuss Jesus than the stars. He only knew enough about astronomy to pass his ranger test.

"Did God make your hair that long?" Rylan interrupted. She was used to seeing men with short hair.

"God did make my hair, but he left it up to me to determine the length. I thought I'd give the Samson look a try," Gabe joked.

The girls looked confused.

"You know, Samson from the Bible? Super strong? Never cut his hair?" Gabe questioned.

"Never heard of him!" Rylan confirmed.

There was a pause. Gabe then asked Emily, "Are you a Christian?"

"I am, but we don't attend church regularly or anything," Emily began to feel more uncomfortable. Maybe the stars were a better topic.

Thankfully, they arrived at her campsite, so the ranger didn't have much opportunity to press the subject further. Rylan was already half asleep.

They said goodnight and he went back to his rounds. Emily snuggled up in her polka dot sleeping bag with Rylan. She thought about how nice it felt to hold her little girl close.

There was something nagging in the back of her mind. *What was it?*

They had eaten a lovely dinner, and-
That's it! Dinner!

The cooler!

She would have to ask the rangers about that tomorrow.

# Chapter 7

*December 23, 2020*

The next morning, Emily woke up to the delicious smell of coffee and a beautiful view of the sun rising over the lake.

"I hope you don't mind drinking your coffee black," a petite woman with shockingly blue eyes said to Emily as she handed her a cup.

"Not at all, thank you," Emily was pleasantly surprised to see several of the church members there with breakfast in tow.

"We figured you'd need some food this morning since your cooler is missing," Lilly explained.

Jolie, the woman who handed Emily the coffee, invited her and Rylan to spend the day with the group.

"We're going to go bird watching and ride the horses to a nearby Amish bakery. We have to pick up our special Christmas cakes for tonight. They'll be closed for the season tomorrow."

"We would love to join you!" Emily surprised everyone, even herself, with her enthusiastic response. "I'm an aspiring baker," she shyly told them. "I've never been to an Amish bakery before. It sounds like a real experience."

"Oh, it is!" Bliss agreed. "I look forward to this part of the trip every year."

Jolie and Lilly raised their eyebrows at Bliss.

"You sure do enjoy it," Jolie snickered.

Bliss rolled her eyes. Emily wanted to ask, but had a feeling she'd find out soon enough.

"We'll be back to pick you up in one hour. I'll get Ranger Boom to hitch up the wagon since we have a little adventurer with us," Lilly winked at Rylan. Emily was again touched at how thoughtful these women are.

Emily and Rylan finished up their delivered breakfast and packed day bags for their upcoming excursion. Emily made sure to have her phone this time.

It seemed like hardly any time passed when an old, rusting black wagon rolled up to campsite number 1. "Property of Agape Poppy" was engraved on the side in big, gold letters. Bliss sat in the driver's seat with Jolie next to her. Lilly was in the back with extra snacks and blankets for Rylan and Emily. Ranger Boom accompanied them on his usual chestnut horse, Chester.

"Miss Irma!" Rylan recognized one of the horses pulling the wagon and immediately went to pet her.

The other horse gave Rylan a nudge, clearly not wanting to be ignored.

"That other one is Louise," Ranger Boom told Rylan.

"Does she like treats, too?" Rylan asked him.

"Oh, yes," Nate nodded.

"I've already given them plenty of treats for the trip out of camp," Lilly warned Rylan, "But you can give them some more when we get back."

Rylan was already excited at the thought of feeling the soft horse lips and coarse hairs tickle the palm of her hand when they got back.

"We'd better get going if we want to see any wildlife," Bliss reminded the group.

"Is it the wildlife we're eager to see?" Lilly asked.

Bliss again ignored the comment. Rylan didn't though.

"Will we see lots of animals?" Rylan asked the ladies.

"I'm sure Ranger Boom can track down a critter or two for you!" Bliss assured Rylan.

Emily and Rylan climbed in the back, but they didn't take off immediately. Instead, Ranger Boom began to pray:

"God, we thank you for this gorgeous morning where we can be together in fellowship and venture out into the amazing world you have created. Please grant us protection as we ride out of the campsite, and let us be a light unto you. Lord, may our steps be worship, may our thoughts be praise, and may our words bring honor to your name. Amen."

Emily never prayed anything like that before. She had thanked God for her blessings and asked for protection, but it had never occurred to her to pray about being a light or to be full of worship. This should be an interesting trip.

The ladies immediately launched into a jumble of chatter and the occasional song as they trotted along the wagon trail. Emily was happy to be lost in her thoughts, she was in a particularly pensive mood. She wondered why Emory hadn't joined them. From their conversation last night, she thought they might make good friends.

"Bobwhite on your left!" Jolie called to the group. Emily looked just in time to see a delicate white head disappear into the brush. She hoped Rylan got a better view.

"What in the world is a bobwhite?" Lilly said in a disapproving tone. She knew Jolie was no avid nature enthusiast and suspected her of making up names.

Jolie sat up straighter and gave her head a proud shake, "It just so happens that a bobwhite is a type of quail. They're very cute."

"I noticed several hawks, too," Ranger Boom told the ladies.

"We'll have to look up more on the way back!" Bliss remarked. She pulled on the reigns to slow down Irma and Louise.

An *incredibly* plain cabin came into view. It was surrounded by big, organized fields that had been carefully prepared for winter. Every edge and line of the cabin was neat and precise, and crisp white curtains hung in the windows. There were at least three vehicles pulled off the side of the main road, their passengers perusing the baked goods for sale inside. Emily could smell gingerbread wafting through the door.

The Agape Poppy campers clambered out of the wagon and made their way into the little shop. There were rows of baked loaves lined up in the middle of the shop. "Mixed berry" seemed to be the most popular heading.

On either end of the room there were cases filled with jars of molasses. The back of the shop featured homemade soaps, and the front had a few hand carved rocking chairs. It was all very simple, clean and straightforward.

Emily wandered around the little bakery while Bliss collected the church's order from the clerk. He brought out four fruitcakes and was happy to hear that Bliss's back was doing better. Apparently, she had purchased a home made salve at their last camping trip and it had "worked wonders".

Rylan found a woman wearing a blue dress and crisp white apron working to set out more jars of molasses.

"Did you make that?" Rylan asked her.

The woman beamed. "I did," she confirmed.

"Is it hard to do?" Rylan pressed.

"Not if you know what you're doing," the woman wisely replied.

"My mom says making stuff in the kitchen is hard."

The woman looked horrified, but her well mannered customs held true and she didn't voice her displeasure that a mother couldn't cook.

Emily heard the conversation and was feeling a little horrified herself.

"You're right, Rylan, mommy did say that," Emily walked up to retrieve her young socialite. "But I do still give cooking and baking an honest effort. Some dishes even turn out edible." She smiled and hoped the church ladies hadn't overheard.

Emily blurted out earlier in the day that she was an aspiring baker. It was true, just emphasis on the aspiring aspect. Her cooking always had excellent flavor; the texture is where she struggled. Things were almost always too runny, too hard, too mushy, etc.

The Amish woman still did not look amused. Thankfully, an eccentric couple joined in the conversation and saved Emily from future embarrassment.

"Edible? I wish that was a word heard in my kitchen!" A woman with wild curly hair and hazel eyes filled with laughter came and stood right next to Emily. She was covered from head to toe in pink attire and managed to fit some butterfly accessories into her outfit, too.

The Amish woman had heard enough and quickly, silently departed. Rylan's attention was completely focused on the pink butterfly woman.

"Are those real butterflies?" Rylan asked her.

"I wish! I've tried wearing flowers before, but the real ones still didn't land on me. Maybe I'll try again in the spring. Do you work here?"

Rylan was delighted at being asked if she worked there. Emily wasn't sure if the woman was joking or not, but then she noticed a cane in her right hand. The woman must be visually impaired. She didn't realize she was talking to a little girl from the city.

"I do work here!" Rylan bounced up and down, thrilled to have a new game.

Emily was about to stop the situation when Lilly touched her shoulder.

"I'd like to see this play out," Lilly whispered to Emily with a smile.

"Is your bread gluten free?" The butterfly woman asked the adorable imposter.

"Nothing is free!" Rylan told her sternly and held up a hand.

The woman didn't seem phased by this reaction. Instead, she proceeded to say, "Not one thing is gluten free? That's a shame, I wanted to try a real Amish item. It's on my adventure list."

Rylan seemed moved by the woman's genuine disappointment.

"Hand massages are free," Rylan told her. She knew she couldn't give away items for free when she didn't really work there, but she could at least give a very relaxing hand massage.

"Hand massage?" The woman looked perplexed for a moment. Surely, this would alert her to the fact that Rylan was not an Amish store clerk.

Then, the woman's face turned to one of complete understanding. "That makes perfect sense!" She exclaimed.

"It does?" Emily questioned. Lilly gave her a "tsk" for interrupting the show.

"Of course," the woman replied to Emily. "They work so much with their hands, it's only natural they would do frequent hand massaging."

The woman turned back in Rylan's direction, "It isn't the cake I had on my adventure list, but it will be a fine substitute. I will happily accept the free hand massage." She extended her hand.

Emily noticed the woman's husband lingering a few feet away. He had a highly amused expression on his face. She wondered if he would ever tell his wife the true story.

Rylan took the woman's hand with both of hers and began expertly rubbing around the wrist in tiny circles with her thumbs. She worked her way down each finger and paid special attention to the pressure point between the pointer finger and thumb.

"What's an adventure list?" Rylan asked her very relaxed 'customer'.

"Oh, you know, the list of adventurous things I want to do in my lifetime," the woman said in a sleepy voice. Rylan's rubbing was taking off some of the excited edge previously present.

"What have you done from your list?"

"Climbed a mountain in Japan, not Fuji, a smaller one. Won a singing competition in London. Successfully entered a cat into a dog show." The woman looked like it was hard to remember everything.

Rylan was buzzing with questions. "What is Japan?"

"A far away place where people look and talk different from here. You should go sometime."

Rylan thought she might just do that.

"How do you get there?"

A frown crossed the woman's face, "I guess it would be difficult for you. You would have to ride a horse a very long way to the ocean and then get on an old fashioned boat. Unless you could convince a whale to swallow you."

"Sounds fun!" Rylan said. "Mom, can we go to Japan?"

Emily was trying her best not to laugh. "I don't know, young lady." She said in mock disapproval. "If we leave, who's going to watch the shop?"

Rylan resumed her role as shopkeeper. "That is a good point. A good worker does not abandon their post!"

"I so admire your dedication!" The woman told her. "I might have to add running a shop to my adventure list."

When the hand massage and conversation concluded, the couple departed the bakery. Emily thought it was a shame they weren't staying at the campsite, they were very entertaining.

"How do you know how to give such good hand massages?" Lilly asked Rylan as they carried fruitcakes to the wagon.

"I massage mom's hands all the time! They get tired from typing. It is our special talk time."

"Clever," Lilly raised an eyebrow at Emily. "I wish I had taught my kids that."

Emily felt embarrassed again. She hadn't taught Rylan how to massage hands for her own benefit.

"It came up when we were playing beauty shop," Emily explained. "She wanted to do everything she saw the real manicurists do."

"Well, I would love a hand massage when we get back to camp!" Lilly told her. "My hands will be tired from making everyone hot chocolate and cutting up these cakes."

The group was packed up in the wagon, eager to get back to Lilly's promised hot chocolate. Emily carefully held onto her designated fruit cake and kept a watchful eye on Rylan's. She would be mortified if they dropped one of the special cakes.

Rylan was starting to get antsy, where was Bliss? They couldn't go anywhere without their designated driver.

Emily's worried eyes met Lilly's.

"She's around the back," Lilly explained.

"Collecting her ornament," Jolie added.

Emily was confused, "I thought the Amish didn't use ornaments?"

"They don't," Jolie replied with a chuckle.

Bliss met William four years ago at the bakery during the church summer camp out. He is a distinguished carpenter in the Amish community and was selling rocking chairs the year they met. His chairs caught her eye because they had a more delicate, decorative flair than the other simple rockers. She commissioned him to make a set of matching chairs for her, her mother, and her sister.

William was intrigued with the passion Bliss put into every detail of her life. It was clear to him that she cared deeply about those around her, just like a mother bear. He carved Bliss a bear ornament and attached it to her chair when she picked the set up that winter.

Every year since, they had come up with some excuse to see each other during the annual camping trips. The Christmas fruit cake errand was one such tradition created for that purpose.

Last year, William gave Bliss a delicately carved feather. She never did figure out the meaning behind that one, but the women did enjoy speculating.

This year, Bliss received an expertly carved bell ornament. The smoothness of the wood always amazed her. How was William able to take something so rough and make it so fine?

"You've just got to keep at it and be patient," he'd told her once when she asked how he'd made the second ornament she received. It was a calf.

Some women might not have wanted the plain bovine carving, but it meant the world to Bliss. She told William the previous year how much joy the spring calves brought to her. She loved to watch them play in the fields around her home. However, she was not a fan of chasing down her many escaping cows. They were surprisingly free spirited for such clunky animals.

"It's a wedding bell, Bliss!" Lilly teased her. The women were back on course to the campsite with Ranger Boom riding close by.

"Y'all know we're just friends!" Bliss blushed. She didn't know how she and William could ever be more than friends. Their lives were very different. Maybe one day things would change; she did hope for that.

"We might need to add in a Spring camping trip," Jolie encouraged her.

"The campground is fun in the spring," Ranger Boom agreed. "Ranger Brooks and I could always use help cataloging the population growth. We have to turn in all kinds of data to the National Parks Association by June 1st."

Emily never realized all the biological work that came with the ranger position. She saw Ranger Brooks and Ranger Boom in a new light.

"I'll bet Miss Rylan here would love to help you count the duck and deer populations," Lilly told Ranger Boom.

"Ducks and deer are so cute!" Rylan agreed.

"That settles it," Jolie declared, "We have to come back in the spring."

Emily might need to get some more camping equipment if this was going to be a regular outing.

The group was singing jingle bells as they pulled into the church camping area.

"Welcome back, sisters!" Ernest called from a group of men relaxing by a fire doing bible study.

"Come get these cakes!" Jolie called back to them.

Soon, everyone was nestled around the campsite with a slice of cake and a glass of hot chocolate. Ranger Boom excused himself to take the horses back to the ranger station. They needed to be fed, groomed, and rested.

Before he slipped off, Rylan reminded him that she was supposed to give the "horsies" a treat.

"That's right!" He smiled. He gave her a handful of oats and made sure her hand was flat and extended for Irma and Louise. The horses happily lapped up the treats and Rylan's giggles filled the whole camp with joy.

The church group entertained one another with tales of various sibling shenanigans. It seems they have some very interesting families.

One man said he used to sneak out of the house every night just to move his brother's car to a weird spot in the yard. It took a whole year for him to get found out.

Emily was happy when Emory emerged from her tent and came to sit with her.

"Did you like the bakery?" Emory asked her in her soft spoken way.

"Yeah, it was pretty plain but riding in the wagon was nice and we met some funny people!" Emily recounted the episode with the eccentric butterfly woman.

"I'll have to put that story in my letters!" Emory laughed. "I didn't go today because it is my letter writing day. I've got people all over the world that I try to keep up with, but I only do it through letters once every four months."

"Why letters?" Emily wondered.

"I don't believe in overusing technology," Emory explained. "I'm not against it, and I definitely do use it, but I don't want it to control my everyday life. I like being able to go through my day without worrying about notifications. I enjoy things a lot more that way."

Emily often thought that a lower tech life might be more enjoyable, but she had never met anyone who actually tried it.

"I think that's really brave of you!" Emily told her. "I'd like to get to that point one day."

"Most people think I'm crazy," Emory seemed to warm up to Emily even more. "I'm glad you see the value in it, too."

Emily and Rylan stayed with the group through dinner. The campers who did not travel to visit the Amish caught a great heap of fish. They happily ate the catch of the day and Lilly was able to make Rylan's seem like chicken. Rylan was at that age where she only wanted chicken or chocolate. Emily hoped the phase passed soon.

Ranger Brooks popped in for dinner, too.

"Do you have my cooler?" Emily quickly asked him as he sat down on the log next to her.

"Hello to you, too," he replied without answering her question.

"Hi, sorry," Emily apologized for jumping ahead. "It's just that, I put a lot into packing that cooler and would really like it back."

"Ranger Boom and I haven't come across any stray coolers," he assured her.

"It must be in the car, then! I can't believe I left it there. Can we go look?" She asked him.

"I don't think it is in your car," Ranger Brooks warned her.

"Why's that? Did you inspect it already?" Emily was annoyed that her theory was being dashed.

"My dog does regularly check the property for suspicious items, and he hasn't shown interest in your car. But, that isn't my reason for believing your cooler isn't in there," the ranger explained.

Emily was intrigued to hear that Ranger Brooks had such a well trained dog, but she pursued the path of the cooler.

"What is your reasoning then, great detective?" She sarcastically pressed.

"I haven't had to chase any bears or raccoons away from the parking lot." Ranger Brooks stated, "The bears would have turned your car over night one if food was in there."

"Bears! Your website didn't say anything about bears," Emily's worries promptly shifted from the cooler to what dangerous wildlife might be lurking in the shadows.

Ranger Brooks happily noticed that she shifted closer to him at the mention of bears.

"The website isn't legally required to disclose anything about bears if there hasn't been a sighting in at least five years," Gabe explained to her.

Emily's attitude immediately reverted back to the offense, "are you telling me that there hasn't been a bear sighting at this campground in at least five years?"

Gabe could tell he had lost.

"Yeah…"

"Then you can't possibly know if my cooler is in the car or not!" Emily accused him. "I'd like to go check." She stood and looked at him expectantly.

The moon and stars were shining brightly tonight. They reflected beautifully in Emily's eyes. Gabe wasn't sure if the light was coming off her or the celestial forces. He'd follow her anywhere.

"Let's go check."

They made a quick stop to tell Lilly they were going to look in the parking lot for Emily's missing cooler.

"I'd be happy to watch Rylan for a bit, if you'd like to go cooler hunting on your own," Lilly offered.

"No, no," Emily protested. "This is our special Christmas trip. Rylan should stay with me,"

"I think she might have more fun here," Lilly persisted. "We are making a Christmas craft."

Emily knew that it'd be easier to look for the cooler without her little princess bouncing around, but she didn't want her to feel left behind.

"Let me ask her," Emily told Lilly. "Be right back," she called to Ranger Brooks.

Emily strode up to Rylan who was nearby collecting an assortment of small sticks.

"Hey, sweetie," Emily started, "do you want to stay and make crafts, or come with mommy to search for the cooler?"

"Crafts!" Rylan eagerly answered.

Emily's spirits soared. Rylan was having fun and making her something. The cooler might soon be found, and Ranger Brooks was waiting to escort her.

Lilly was thrilled to get to spend some quality time with Rylan. As soon as she met the little girl, she could tell they were kindred spirits.

"Did you get your mom anything for Christmas?" Lilly asked her.

Rylan looked concerned. "No, I usually figure something out the night before."

"Sometimes it is nice to be prepared!" Lilly encouraged her, "Maybe we should make her something now. That way you can relax later."

Rylan was impressed that Lilly knew how to make more time for relaxing. But she didn't know how they could make anything in the middle of the woods.

"I don't even have my crayons," Rylan lamented.

"I've got some craft supplies," Lilly informed her. "We've also got plenty of sticks and pine needles."

Rylan thought that was an understatement. She thought they had more sticks and pine needles than anyone else in the whole world. She had already collected some interesting looking ones.

"Do you always have everything you need?" Rylan wondered after they started working on the present.

"Not always," Lilly admitted. "I've become better at being prepared as I got old."

"What were you like before you got old?" Rylan asked. She was excited to get information from a real old person and not just a slightly old person pretending to be really old.

"I was a little different," Lilly reflected. "I used to be afraid of people."

"My mom is afraid of people," Rylan confessed.

"People can be scary," Lilly confirmed. "I used to watch them and not talk to them. I was afraid I would do or say something wrong and make them upset."

"How did you get unafraid?" Rylan was intrigued.

"I started reading the bible." Lilly said. "I didn't always understand it at first. Sometimes things would happen and then I would read a bible verse that would suddenly make sense. The verse that helped me not be afraid of people was 2 Timothy 1:7 and 8."

"What did it say/" Rylan was bubbling with curiosity now.

Lilly paraphrased as best she could remember the verse, "God's spirit does not give us fear, but gives us power, love, and self control to share the good news of Christ."

"What is the good news?" Rylan wondered.

Lilly shared with Rylan how Jesus was born to save everyone who chose to believe in him and follow his teachings.

Rylan knew bits and pieces of the story already, and she really liked the part about angels, but she still didn't understand how the verse helped Lilly not be afraid.

Lilly knew the conversation started out with questions about being prepared. She tried to get back on track, "When you love Jesus like I do, you love all the people like he does. That means you try to be the best you can so that when those people need you, you can help. So I had to start being ready. Part of that was overcoming my fears to talk to people. You can't make Christmas crafts with someone if you're afraid of them."

"How does making a craft help someone?" Rylan really is observant for a seven year old child.

"It plants a seed," Lilly smiled. She loved answering questions. She told Rylan all about how seeds grow and what they need to thrive.

# Chapter 8

"Ready?" Emily and Gabe were about to go search for her missing cooler.

They set off with flashlights on. They followed a path Emily hadn't been on before. It was the main entrance to campsite number 2 that split off the main trail. The path she had been using to go between campsites was a newer addition, part of the "Agape Lake Trail." Currently, they were heading to the officially named "Base Camp Trail."

"Why is this cooler so important to you?" Gabe asked her as they strode down the path.

"Several reasons," Emily replied. "For one, I spent a lot of time researching the best coolers and spent quite a bit of money on this one. Secondly, I worked really hard to season the food inside. I'm not the best chef in the world, but I do enjoy making my own spice blends. I spent days leading up to this trip experimenting with different campfire roast recipes to get the right mix of herbs. I was actually excited to try them. On our other trips we've always gone out to eat, this was my big chance to do the cooking."

She glanced at Gabe to see if he was bored and he gave her an encouraging smile.

She continued, "Rylan and I have always dreamed of owning our own shop of some kind. She envisions a toy shop, I tend to lean towards a bakery."

"But you aren't a good cook?" Gabe questioned.

"Not the best, no, but I do think I did well with the homemade seasonings. If I find the cooler, I'll prove it to you."

"I believe you," he assured her. "I was just wondering if bakery is a good idea. Sounds to me like you should have a spice shop."

"It's a nice thought, I've investigated that possibility. The problem is most successful spice shops grow their own herbs, I do not have a green thumb."

Gabe wanted to tell her that he would go into business with her and grow anything she wanted, but he held himself back. This was just their second walk, after all.

Instead he casually mentioned, "I have a garden."

"You do?" Emily was surprised he had time to garden. It seemed these rangers were pretty busy. "How do you find the time?"

Gabe seized the opportunity to make an herb joke about thyme, "I always plant it alphabetically, between the tarragon and turmeric."

Emily couldn't help but laugh at his quick thinking. Then she wondered if he really planted alphabetically. Before she could ask, he answered her previous question seriously.

"I find it is easy to take care of something I care about." The Ranger stared straight at her when he made this statement.

His words made Emily blush. She allowed herself to look at him directly in the face, something she usually avoided doing. There was something so gentle there.

She tried to get back to their conversation. What had they been discussing? Taking care of something?

*Not taking care of you, silly.* She told herself.

Gardening! Right.

"What, um, what plants are in your garden?" She stammered.

"After we check your car, would you like to see? It's in the courtyard of the Ranger Station." They were walking so closely now that their arms brushed. Emily was very aware of his great height.

She wasn't sure she wanted to be alone with him in the Ranger Station, it was, after all, only their second walk. "Will Ranger Boom be there?" She asked.

"And the park manager," he confirmed.

"Oh, good, I can tell the manager all about how you misdiagnosed my cooler problem!" She joked.

"We're about to find out who the wrong one is," he pointed in front of them, "there's your car."

Emily walked up to her trunk, "Drumroll, please!"

She dramatically flung open the trunk.

It was empty!

Emily quickly looked through the rest of the vehicle.

Empty. Empty. Empty.

Did she really leave it at home?

Emily dejectedly closed all the car doors and then the trunk. Gabe let his hand rest on hers.

"We all forget things sometimes," he tried to console her.

Tears began to form in Emily's eyes. "I try, but I always forget something or do something wrong."

"You also do lots of things right," he reminded her.

"I do?" She sniffled.

"You're very kind to your daughter, you work hard, you try new things," he rattled off.

"You only just met me, you don't know any of that for sure," her tears were beginning to abate.

"My intuition is usually right," he smiled. "Ready to go see the garden?"

"Just a quick tour," Emily said. "I'm ready to get back to my tent."

Ranger Brooks led her into the station. They walked past the front desk and a little break room, then came to a side door. He opened the door on a beautiful scene.

A woman with long wavy brown hair sat in the middle of a courtyard next to a fire and a gently bubbling fountain. Tiny, soft orange lights were woven around the garden beds. The woman's seat looked to be an older model of one of the Amish rockers Emily saw earlier in the day. Three other such rockers circled the fire-fountain centerpiece. Gabe and Emily sat down to her right.

Emily's tearful mood from the parking lot faded away the moment she saw this serene spot. She gave the woman her biggest smile and waved hello.

"Welcome to our Ranger Garden," the woman said to Emily. "Are you enjoying
your stay? I'm the park manager, Pam."

Emily's mind immediately jumped back to her emails and she felt a rush of guilt. She forgot to bring the can of food Pam requested for the Christmas food drive. Emily tried to remember that at least Pam didn't know she had forgotten.

"I actually am enjoying myself," Emily told her brightly. Maybe she could make up for not bringing a can by spreading some joy, "Ranger Brooks and Ranger Boom have been very helpful."

"I am always glad to hear my boys are doing a good job," Pam winked at Gabe.

"Thanks, Mom," Ranger Brooks replied.

*Mom!* That sneaky ranger. She was already meeting his mother and they hadn't even gone on a first date. Emily should have realized they are related. They have the same last name.

"You're staying at campsite one, aren't you? By the lake?" Pam asked Emily.

"Yes! It's beautiful, you maintain an amazing park." Emily told her.

"Most of the credit goes to Nate and Gabe," Pam confided. "They work very hard to keep things clean and safe for our guests."

"I actually brought Emily here to show her some of the edible plants we grow in the courtyard. She has a special interest in cooking."

"Make sure she sees the tea section, I'll bet she loves tea!" Pam urged him.

Emily found herself wanting to ask about Pam's dream she overheard Nate and Gabe discussing when they were leading her to the campsite the day before, but she didn't want to create an awkward situation if it was supposed to be private.

Gabe walked Emily around the little garden showing off his various plants. They ended at the "tea" section where a pretty yellow teapot sat on a stand surrounded by prayer rocks.

"What's your favorite tea?" Gabe asked Emily as he knelt to one knee.

"Mint," Emily replied, a little embarrassed at the simplicity. Should she have lied and said something more exotic?

"I like that one, too," Gabe said as he clipped off some mint leaves. He pulled a little bag from a stash inside the tea pot, filled it with the mint clippings, and handed it to Emily. "Tomorrow, your morning will be minty fresh."

"Thank you!" Emily happily took the tea bag and wasn't sure if she would ever use it. She might just put it in her keepsake drawer at home. This was a night she wanted to remember, even with her cooler still missing.

They said goodnight to Pam. Gabe led her to the stables where Ranger Boom was about to head out on his patrol with Chester.

"Hey, Nate," Gabe called out to the other ranger, "will you take Emily back to campsite two?"

"Sure thing!" Nate answered.

Gabe helped Emily get up onto Chester and waved as they rode away.

Emily was unsure about riding so close to Nate on the big brown horse, but she soon realized there was nothing to worry about. Nate had one of those easy going natures that made everyone feel comfortable.

"Did you have a good evening?" Nate asked her as Chester plodded over the uneven path.

"Surprisingly good," Emily confirmed. "But I am bursting to know what Pam's dream was about," she admitted.

"Oh, you heard that? It's really nothing serious," Nate replied. He decided he'd better tell Emily about the dream just as a way to pass the time. He didn't want any awkward silence. "Pam has been dreaming that she builds a house and then it falls down. Sometimes it is easy to build, but sometimes it is hard. The falling isn't consistent, either. In last week's dream it fell down immediately, but this week it fell after several years."

"How could a house stand for several years in just one dream?" Emily wondered out loud.

"Timing in dreams is just funny like that," Nate shrugged. "I've been trying to figure out what it means, but I'm not having much luck."

Emily thought for awhile about building a house only to have it fall. Maybe Pam is insecure about something. She's definitely worried.

When they arrived back at the church campsite, Emily said goodnight to Nate and made her way over to Lilly.

"No cooler." Emily said with an air of defeat.

"Hopefully, you still found something?" Lilly said with a twinkle in her eye.

Emily wondered if there had been talk about her and Ranger Brooks. "I met the park manager," Emily said tentatively.

"Oh, meeting the mother is a great start!" Lilly cheerfully replied. "Rylan and I had a great time, too."

Rylan bounced up to Emily, "I finished your Christmas present, mommy!"

"Yay!" Emily smiled and clapped for Rylan, "where is it?"

"Uh uh," Rylan shook her head, "you have to wait for Christmas."

"Okay, my little Christmas elf!" Emily picked up Rylan and gave her cheek a nuzzle. "Time for us to get back to our camp."

"See you tomorrow!" Lilly told Emily.

She bid the other campers goodnight and followed the now familiar lake trail back to her own tent. Rylan chattered the whole way about their day. She really enjoyed the wagon ride, seeing the Amish bakery, and making Emily's mysterious Christmas present.

"Mom, will you ever really open your own bakery?" Rylan asked her.

"Maybe not a bakery, but someday I do think we'll be able to open up our own shop. Especially if we can figure out what kind of shop it will be."

"I hope our shop is prettier than the one we visited today," Rylan yawned.

"I thought you liked the one we saw today," Emily said, surprised.

"It was good, but I want ours to have lots of butterflies and colors."

"That would be nice," Emily allowed her mind to picture a cozy little store scene as she drifted off to sleep.

"Can't sleep yet, mom!"

"What? Why not?"

"We have to say prayers," Rylan told her.

Emily should have known that spending so much time with the church group would rub off on them.

"Okay, sweetie, I'll start. Dear God, thank you for this day and for this beautiful camp. Thank you for surrounding us with good, helpful people and for blessing us with this time together. Please help us to honor you this Christmas season and continue to open our hearts to your love and guidance. In Jesus' name we pray, Amen."

"Amen," Rylan snuggled into her mom and went to sleep.

Praying stirred Emily's conscience and was making it hard for her to sleep. She had so many things to think about!

She finally focused her thoughts on the lake that lay just outside their tent. She imagined herself drifting around in a canoe while listening to Rylan sing silly songs. That image put her into a deep, happy sleep.

# Chapter 9

December 24, 2020

Emily woke up to her phone constantly buzzing.

She sleepily reached passed Rylan and found the nagging device.

"Hello?" She whispered into the microphone.

Static.

She hung the phone up and decided she would check messages after breakfast. The church group had packed up a breakfast basket for them to use that morning and invited them to come over for lunch around 12:30 pm.

Emily started a fire and got breakfast going. She took a moment to admire Agape lake. It wasn't as beautiful as a waterfall, but it was still peaceful. In fact, it was just what she needed. Being forced to find beauty in the lake opened Emily's mind up to other opportunities.

The sun was almost up and several birds swooped around the waters. She needed to ask the rangers for a bird watching book. It would be nice to know what she was looking at.

Rylan joined her by the fire and nibbled on one of the banana muffins from the basket.

"Good morning, Princess," Emily greeted her with a hug.

"Morning, mommy," Rylan nuzzled into her. She was always her snuggliest in the morning.

"What are we doing today?" Rylan asked Emily as she rubbed some sleep from her eyes.

"I'm not sure yet," Emily admitted.

"We could take a boat ride on the lake," Rylan suggested. She heard some of the other campers talking about boats yesterday and it sounded like fun.

"It would be dangerously cold if we fell in," Emily surmised. Hypothermia was not on her camping list.

"We could go on a treasure hunt," some of Rylan's usual enthusiastic energy was coming alive.

Emily remembered the conversation they had before they left for the camping trip.

"Are we looking for the treasure those wild raccoons stole from us?" She joked.

"Yes!" Rylan yelled, "We have to get it back. There's special medicine inside the treasure box that Lena needs!"

"Who is Lena? And why does she need medicine?" Emily always enjoyed trying to keep up with Rylan's imagination.

"Ugh! Don't you know Lena?" Rylan threw her hands up. "She is the ducky living right over there," Rylan pointed to the lake. Emily's eyes followed the finger's direction until her gaze rested on a happy brown and blue wood duck swimming close to the shore.

"She's beautiful! Nice to meet you, Lena," to Emily's surprise, the duck quacked back and shook it's tail.

"She wants you to go find the treasure box so she can have her medicine," Rylan reminded Emily.

"Oh, right. What sort of medicine is it?"

"Sweet medicine to help her head," Rylan whispered. "She has a headache."

"Poor duck! You don't have a headache too, do you Rylan?" Emily wanted to make sure her daughter wasn't sending her some kind of message through her game.

"Nope! I'm great, I'm just ready to go find the treasure."

Emily wasn't sure how she could hide a treasure chest with duck headache medicine in it while also looking for that same chest with her very observant daughter watching. She also needed to check her messages. It could have been her boss calling earlier.

Emily didn't take much vacation time and was always worried about the office when she did. As one of only three employees, she was responsible for a huge chunk of the daily operations, including finances. The job was definitely stressful at times, especially when the board of directors wanted answers. Right now, the board was reviewing the group's 2019-2020 audit report. The report was clean, but somehow there was still some "knit-picking." Emily was not a fan of explaining all the minute details over and over again.

Emily told Rylan to make up a special treasure hunt song and map to help them find the treasure chest. This bought her more time to figure out what to hide.

She was listening to Rylan hum the "map" song from the hit kid's show "Dora the Explorer" and staring at her suitcase when she heard a familiar banjo tune on the breeze.

*Oh beautiful star of Bethlehem*
*Shine upon us until the glory dawn*
*Give us a lamp to light the way*
*Unto the land of perfect day*
*Oh beautiful star of Bethlehem shine on*

Jamey and Kenaniah paraded into campsite 1 with smiles on and voices blaring.

"Good morning!" Kenaniah called out to them.

Emily was relieved to see them, their arrival would give her more time to figure out the treasure hunt.

"Hello!" She waved back.

"We brought you some snacks," Jamey said as Kenaniah passed a snack bag to Emily.

*Perfect!* This could be the treasure.

"Actually," Emily pushed the bag back towards him, "would you mind burying it under the 10th tree on the left down the lake trail?"

"Um...okay, not a problem," Jamey replied with his usual non intrusive nature.

Kenaniah was more curious. "Why?" He questioned.

Emily hastily explained about the treasure hunt and encouraged them to slip away quickly before Rylan came over. She was currently deeply invested in the drawing of her treasure map.

The boys hurried back the way they came, concealing the treat bag and resuming their song.

A quack from Lena alerted Rylan to the present and she noticed Jamey and Kenaniah leaving.

"Did they not want to go on the treasure hunt with us?" Rylan asked Emily.

"They had to go sing Christmas songs to the other campers," Emily hoped this wasn't a complete lie.

"I thought we were the only other campers?" Rylan continued.

*She really is observant!* Emily thought. "I think there are other campers in a different part of the park, maybe on the other side of the lake? They use RVs instead of tents, so they can't camp in this section."

This answer seemed to satisfy Rylan, but she wasn't done thinking about Jamey and Kenaniah. "Can we go with them?" She wondered. "I like singing, we could do our treasure hunt later."

Emily wanted to give the musicians a chance to hide the treat bag, "Not right now, sweetie," she said. "I need to do some work. You stay right here, I'm going to walk around to get a cell signal."

Emily left Rylan playing by the tent with Lena while she walked a little ways down the "Base Camp Trail" trying to get cell service.

She was finally able to get enough coverage to listen to her voicemail, it was, indeed, her boss, Janet.

"Oh Emily, Emily, I hope you're having a wonderful time on your trip. I was just calling to congratulate you on your fine work and to offer you a position as the finance director. The board will, of course, want to do an official interview, but you should pass that easily. Call me back so we can discuss!"

Emily couldn't believe she was being offered a promotion. She knew the budget was already spread thin, would they be increasing her salary? Or was this just a tricky title change to get her to do more work?

Janet wasn't the type to be tricky. She was a very fair person. *There must be a new revenue stream.* Emily's interest was very piqued.

Emily started to head back to her tent, content to return Janet's call after Christmas. That didn't mean she wouldn't be thinking about it, though.

As Emily walked down the path, she heard an unfamiliar voice softly singing "I wonder as I wander." It stirred deep emotions in her. Her grandfather always used to sing that song around Christmas time. She felt his loss keenly.

Emily closed her eyes and listened to the song progress, remembering sitting in her grandpa's lap and being rocked to sleep.

*I wonder as I wander out under the sky,*
*How Jesus the Savior did come for to die.*
*For poor on'ry people like you and like I*

*When Mary birthed Jesus 'twas in a cow's stall,*
*With wise men and farmers and shepherds and all.*
*But high from God's heaven a star's light did fall,*
*And the promise of ages it then did recall.*

*If Jesus had wanted for any wee thing,*
*A star in the sky, or a bird on the wing,*
*Or all of God's angels in heav'n for to sing,*
*He surely could have it, 'cause he was the King.*

*I wonder as I wander out under the sky,*
*How Jesus the Savior did come for to die.*
*For poor on'ry people like you and like I*
*I wonder as I wander out under the sky.*

When the song ended, Emily opened her eyes and realized she had been away from Rylan longer than intended. She needed to hurry back and get the treasure hunt going. She was thankful the treat bag was hidden on the way to the church group, they'd be needing lunch soon.

She rushed into camp, still wondering who had been singing the song, and was surprised to see Ranger Brooks walking past her tent.

"Hey!" She shouted to him from the trail entrance.

He turned, waved, and strode towards her.
"A fine morning, isn't it?"

"It is!" Emily was feeling a little overwhelmed, but aware of how many blessings she had already received that day. "Was that you singing?"

The ranger blushed. He didn't know anyone could hear him

through the trees.
"Yeah, that's one of my favorites."

"Mine too," she happily noted.

"Where's Rylan?" He asked her.

"Oh she's just playing over here by the water," Emily walked around the other side of the tent.

Rylan wasn't there.

Emily checked inside the tent, she wasn't there either. She fought the panic creeping up inside her.

"She's missing," Emily choked out as she continued to look around the campsite.

"Maybe she went over to the church camp?" Ranger Brooks offered. He was used to children wandering off at the camp, especially if they had friends nearby. "Let's not get worried until we check there."

They walked in silence down the trail leading to campsite 2. Emily watched and listened carefully for any trace of Rylan.

Ranger Brooks was also staying alert, but his heart was calling out to God on behalf of Emily and Rylan. Begging for the little girl to be safe and found quickly.

*"In the same way, the Spirit comes to help our weakness. We don't know what we should pray, but the Spirit himself pleads our case with unexpressed groans."*
*Romans 8:26 CEB*

# Chapter 10

"Why did we pick *Star of Bethlehem* to sing today?" Kenaniah asked Jamey as they made their way to the RV side of the campground.

"During this morning's devotional, Brother Ernest read to us about the wise men seeing the star in the East. It got me thinking about God guiding us on our individual journeys." Jamey answered him.

That morning, the pastor pointed out that the star did not guide the wise men for most of their journey. The star was a sign the wise men had been looking for, but they still had to travel a great distance based on faith.

"What journey?" Kenaniah felt lost on the subject. He had slept through the morning devotional.

"Life's journey," Jamey continued. "You know, God made each of us for a special purpose. It's our job to pay attention to the gifts, desires, and opportunities God has blessed us with so that we can follow the path he designed for us."

"How are we supposed to know if we're on the right path?" Kenaniah wondered.

"That part can be difficult, I think," Jamey explained. "It's especially hard to decipher your turning points when you aren't in a season of prayer and bible study. But, one way to know if you're doing the right thing is by asking yourself 'Does this glorify God?' If the answer is a clear 'yes', then chances are you're on the 'right path'."

"I do remember a sermon about confusion coming from the enemy," Kenaniah added.

"Right. If you're confused, you might want to slow down and pray for clarity before making any major decisions," Jamey confirmed.

"There's no way everyone always makes the right choice, though," Kenaniah's mind was really digging into the subject.

"That's where God's artistry and amazing grace come into play," Jamey reminded him.

Kenaniah thought about all the tales of redemption he had heard. God really could turn around any situation.

"That reminds me of Linda making spaghetti," Kenaniah reminisced.

"What?" Jamey had no idea where this was going.

"You remember! In bible school, whenever we would mess up our pictures, Linda would help us turn the mistake into a bowl of spaghetti." Kenaniah smiled at the memory. He wondered how many sloppily drawn scenes of Jesus feeding the 5,000 had hidden bowls of spaghetti in them.

Jamey smiled, too. Linda had helped him draw many bowls of spaghetti. Sometimes, he even made a mistake on purpose to see if it could be "spaghettified." It always could.

The boys sang "Beautiful Star of Bethlehem" with a new passion that day. They even wrote a new song about God's guidance that night.

They entered RV campsite number 6 and weren't ready for the curve ball that came at them. Literally.

"Sorry! Are you okay?" A teenage boy with thick, dark hair came running up to where Jamey lay.

"Leaping Lazarus!" Kenaniah shrieked, "He's dead!"

"Oh my mom is going to be so mad," the teenager wailed.

"Arise, sweet friend! The grave can't have you yet!" Kenaniah shouted.

"I'm fine, I'm fine," Jamey mumbled.

"A miracle!" Kenaniah kissed his hands and stretched them heavenward.

"I didn't die!" Jamey protested.

"No, but we're all about to wish we were dead," the other ball player came up to the group. "Looks like that ball went straight through Old Jed's RV window."

The ball would surely have smashed into Jamey's head if he hadn't dropped so quickly. The weight of the banjo made him fall a little harder than intended, making it difficult for him to get back up. He would be adding that moment to his testimony. He never saw the ball coming for him. He believed an angel pushed him down, saving him from a nasty accident.

As the laws of physics say, an object in motion stays in motion. That ball continued past the spot where Jamey had stood and went crashing through "Old Jed's" RV window.

"Now hold on, we weren't involved in any of this," Jamey reminded the younger boys. We just came to sing some carols and invite everyone to a Candlelight service by the lake."

"Maybe Jed won't be mad," the younger teen hoped.

"Are you crazy?" The older one argued,"Last year he sued my grandma for stepping on his squash garden."

"The situation does seem bleak," Jamey agreed with the older teen. "By the way, I'm Jamey and this is Kenaniah," he reached out for a handshake.

"I'm Isaiah," the older and bigger of the two replied and returned the handshake.

"I'm DJ," the younger one waved.

"Well, Isaiah, DJ, you might want to find this Mr. Jed and tell him what happened. It might make him less angry if you tell him immediately."

"He's away buying horses," DJ said dejectedly.

"Do you want to come caroling with us while you wait for him to get back?" Kenaniah offered.

The teens shrugged in agreement. After all, continuing their ball game seemed ill advised after the incident.

The boys quickly reviewed which carols they all knew and walked over to a group of fishermen (and women) while singing "What Child is This."

*This, this is Christ the King,*
*Whom shepherds guard and Angels sing*
*Haste, haste, to bring Him laud,*
*The Babe,*
*The Son,*
*Of Mary.*

"Shh! You'll scare the fish!" An older woman with long Christmas tree earrings gave the boys a disapproving look.

"Oh, Ethel, don't be so serious!" One of her companions chided. "I like the carols. Especially that one. Did you know I got baptized in this very lake forty years ago because of that song?"

"Yes, Ruthie, I was here," Ethel sighed and sat back. She knew what was coming.

"It's just such a good story!" Ruthie beamed. "Would you boys like to hear it?"

"Yes ma'am!" They eagerly agreed and sat down closer to Ruthie so they could enjoy her tale.

"I'll start for you, dear," Ethel told Ruthie. To the newcomers, she added, "Ruthie tends to tell the long version if I don't start her off on Christmas Day." The ladies shared a look and Ethel continued.

"Ruthie and her son came camping with me and my son on Christmas break in 1980. She and I had our hair permed the day before we left on the camping trip, so we didn't want our boys getting us wet with lake water."

"Water ruins perms," Ruthie added.

"Completely," Ethel agreed.

"It is unpleasant enough to get wet in the winter, anyways," Ruthie continued.

"That's precisely why we should have left your prankster child at home!" Ethel remarked.

"Your boy is just as bad!" Ruthie retorted.

The middle aged men that were fishing nearby high fived. One of them called out, "Don't let her give us a bad name, mom!"

"They still prank us, you know," Ethel whispered to her little audience.

"Oh, yes," Ruthie agreed. "Yesterday, Edwin switched out my mud mask with real mud."

"And Eden ate all of the cookies," Ethel lamented.

"That isn't a prank!" Ruthie declared.

"No, but it was disappointing," Ethel shrugged. "Anyways, we were all out here camping and our hair looked fabulous."

"But then the boys dumped a bucket of water on us," Ruthie interjected.

"Then our hair didn't look so fabulous," Ethel admitted.

"We didn't feel fabulous, either," Ruthie ominously said. "We contracted horrible colds."

"We had to be rushed to the ranger station by horse wagon. Thankfully, there was a handsome doctor there who saved our lives and Ruthie's soul," Ethel put her hand over her heart.

"I believe his name was Leroy," Ruthie picked the story back up. "Ethel was already a Christian. I used to make fun of her for believing in such nonsense. But while I was coughing and chilling in that ranger station, I came to realize it was certainly not nonsense. That song you were singing, *What Child Is This*, played on the doctor's radio. I asked him what on earth "laud" meant. He told me it meant to praise or worship, and I said why would you want to make haste to praise someone? He said because when you love someone, you want to tell them, and you want to tell them immediately. That got me thinking about love. I loved my son and told him all the time. In fact, I told him I loved him the second he was born. He didn't even know what I was saying, but I was overflowing with so much love I had to tell him."

Ruthie paused to wipe a tear from her eye. Her silly mood from earlier had abated and you could feel the love and passion emanating from her heart as she shared her testimony.

"The doctor told me that the man who wrote *What Child is This*, William Dix, was sick, too, just like me. He said in those moments when William didn't know if he'd survive or not, all he wanted to do was tell Jesus how much he loved him. In that moment, I could really feel how much Jesus loves me. It was overwhelming. The doctor prayed with me that day. I admitted that I am a sinner, professed that I believe Jesus is God's son, and decided I would confess publicly that he died to save me from sin."

Ethel clapped, "She did her ABC's!"

"Her ABC's?" Isaiah repeated, puzzled.

"Admit. Believe. Confess." Jamey explained. "It is the easiest way for new believers to repent of their sins and accept Jesus as their savior. It comes directly from scripture."

The wheels of Ethel's well studied mind began to turn, she recited Romans 10: 9-10:

"Because if you confess with your mouth "Jesus is Lord" and in your heart you have faith that God raised him from the dead, you will be saved. Trusting with the heart leads to righteousness, and confessing with the mouth leads to salvation."

Ruthie nodded, "And confess publicly I did! I began attending church with Ethel and learned more about what it means to be a Christian. We returned to Agape Lake that summer with the church and I was baptized in front of everyone."

"Where does baptism fall into the ABC's?" DJ asked her.

"It provides a format for you to declare your faith publicly, and symbolizes that the old you has died and you are reborn in Christ. It also gives you great power and authority." Ethel answered him.

"Power and authority?" This was new to Isaiah.

"Absolutely," Ruthie confirmed. "The Holy Spirit enters you when you are baptized. It gives you comfort, guidance, and the authority of Christ over evil. You have the power to shun all evil. All you have to do is believe and speak it."

Talking with the women gave the boys a lot to think about. Jamey extended the invite for them to attend the candlelight service that evening and they readily accepted.

"Ready to go spread some more Christmas cheer?" Kenaniah asked Isaiah and DJ as they walked back towards the RVs.

"I think we'd better go figure out how to pay for that window," DJ said.

"And I'd like to go read my bible," Isaiah admitted.

"Maybe we'll see you tonight!" Jamey waved and led Kenaniah on to the next group of campers.

# Chapter 11

"Excuse me, campers!" Ranger Brooks called out to the church group milling about campsite 2.

He and Emily emerged from the lake trail and made their way to the fire pit. The others joined them there.

"Has anyone seen Rylan today?" Ranger Brooks asked the group.

He was greeted with several "no's" and worried head shakes. He could feel Emily shaking next to him. He had to fight to control his own growing concern. He had been sure Rylan was at the church camp.

"Has anyone noticed anything out of the ordinary today?" The ranger addressed the group again.

Bliss spoke up, "I heard quite a bit of meowing this morning."

"Do you know about what time and which direction the meowing occurred?" The ranger questioned.

Bliss carefully thought back, "it was sometime after breakfast. Really not that long ago. Hard to say which direction it was coming from."

Sally spoke to Ranger Brooks, "I remember the meowing, too, I think it came from the lake trail. It was just before you walked through on your rounds."

"That must have been what made Rylan run off, she loves cats!" Emily started to rush back down the lake trail. Gabe grabbed her arm to stop her.

"You need to stay at your tent in case Rylan comes back," he told her firmly. "I'll get Ranger Boom to sit with you so we can send radio updates."

"We'll turn our radio on, too," Lilly assured Emily. "If Rylan comes through here, we'll call."

"God is in control," Ernest said. He immediately began to pray.

Ranger Brooks took off down the lake trail. It wound around the entire lake perimeter, past Emily's tent and to the RV section. Several of the church members fanned out to search the woods and the base camp trail.

Bliss and Jolie followed Emily back to her campsite. They didn't want her to be alone during such a difficult time. Ranger Boom joined them within minutes.

Bliss tried to break the tension, "Does anyone want hot tea? I've got a few bags in my satchel."

"Tea would be nice," Jolie agreed.

"I'll get the fire started," Ranger Boom offered. He stood up to find some wood.

"I'll help," Emily sniffled. She hadn't stopped crying since she discovered Rylan wasn't at the church camp.

"No, no, you rest here," Bliss told her. She was worried about the young mother.

"I don't want to rest!" Emily wailed. "I just want to find my little girl!" She doubled over and dug her nails into the dirt.

In her despair, Emily couldn't help but wonder if she made a mistake when she adopted Rylan. Not because she didn't want her, but because she doubted if she was the best choice of mother.

This wasn't the first time she had doubted herself, but it was the most valid. The child she swore to care for was missing. The layers of guilt, worry, and doubt were weighing so heavy on Emily that she could hardly breathe.

If she had been alone in that moment, there's no telling what she might have done. The enemy loves to take advantage of the isolated.

Jolie knelt down beside her and rubbed her back. "You did help," she whispered to Emily. "You did."

"That's right," Bliss added, making sure her tone was soft. "You knew she would follow the cat meowing."

"And Rylan will be so happy to see you here at the tent when she gets back," Jolie assured her.

The somber group allowed Emily time to cry while they prayed for the speedy recovery and safety of the missing child.

"I wish I had never left her alone," Emily whispered. She was trying to keep a happy image of Rylan in her mind so she wouldn't start crying again, but it was hard not to retrace all the ways she had messed up. It seemed like all she knew how to do was mess up.

Bliss stoked the fire Nate had just built and put a kettle on. "That does seem out of character for you, what happened?"

"I wasn't thinking clearly," Emily admitted. "Rylan wanted to play a treasure hunt game. I was trying to figure out how to go about it, but I couldn't stop thinking about work. My phone rang early this morning and I was afraid there was a problem at the office. I slipped away to check my messages and when I got back she was gone."

"You have a stressful job, don't you?" Jolie said sympathetically.

"It isn't my dream job and it does require some overtime, but I mostly enjoy it." Emily answered. "The message I listened to was actually from my boss. She told me I might get a promotion."

Bliss's face was full of concern, "Won't a promotion mean even longer hours?"

"Maybe," Emily felt defensive. "I haven't been told the specifics yet. But if there's more money involved, I could do so much more for Rylan."

"But you don't know if you'd have the time to do more for her," Bliss reminded her.

Jolie recalled her own days of labor, "I used to try working my way to happiness. It was difficult to find a good balance."

"You've got to save time for God and family," Bliss agreed.

"We can fit some time in for God now," Ranger Boom offered. "I've got my bible right here." He pulled out a worn, leather pocket bible. He hoped reading some scripture would calm everyone's nerves.

*"What do workers gain from all their hard work? I have observed the task that God has given human beings. God has made everything fitting in its time, but has also placed eternity in their hearts, without enabling them to discover what God has done from beginning to end. I know that there's nothing better for them but to enjoy themselves and do what's good while they live. Moreover, this is the gift of God: that all people should eat, drink, and enjoy the results of their hard work. I know that whatever God does will last forever; it's impossible to add to it or take away from it. God has done this so that people are reverent before him. Whatever happens has already happened, and whatever will happen has already happened before. And God looks after what is driven away."*
*Ecclesiastes 3:9-15 CEB*

Emily wasn't listening. She felt so beaten. Rylan was missing, the church ladies were questioning her promotion, and now the ranger wanted to do bible study. Perhaps, if Emily had opened her heart and mind she would have received comfort, but that was not the case.

"I don't think I'm in the right frame of mind for bible study," Emily turned towards the lake and wished the others would leave her alone.

"That's exactly when you need God the most," Jolie told her.

"Talking to God is the only way I can get calmed down," Bliss put in.

Ranger Boom wasn't ready to give up, he turned to Mathew 11:28, *"Come to Me, all you who labor and are heavy laden, and I will give you rest. Take My yoke upon you and learn from Me, for I am gentle and lowly in heart, and you will find rest for your souls. For My yoke is easy and My burden is light."*

"Bible study doesn't work for me," Emily insisted.

"Maybe you just need to get to know God a little better," Ranger Boom rested his hand on his bible. He was all too familiar with people not having faith in God. "Sometimes he works in our lives differently than we expect."

Jolie thought of her own faith journey, "I used to think God wasn't answering my prayers. Then I realized he was guiding me right where I needed to be, even though I had some heartache."

"That's right," Bliss couldn't hide her own tears anymore. "God brought me to his peace and church family by putting me through some heart ache. I had to experience his amazing grace to finally understand the truth."

Despite her own sorrow, Emily was moved by the tearful display. She decided to give the Bible study a chance.

Ranger Boom began reading again and the ladies joined hands.

*"And He said to me, "My grace is sufficient for you, for My strength is made perfect in weakness." Therefore most gladly I will rather boast in my infirmities, that the power of Christ may rest upon me. Therefore I take pleasure in infirmities, in reproaches, in needs, in persecutions, in distresses, for Christ's sake. For when I am weak, then I am strong."*

*II Corinthians 12:9-10*

# Chapter 12

Rylan was playing by the tent waiting on her mom to come back from her phone calls. She was proud of her mom for working so hard.

She used a purple crayon to draw a very zig-zagging line around the picture of the campsite she made.

"This is the path we need to follow to find the treasure," Rylan told her duck friend, Lena.

*Quack, quack.*

"I know it goes back and forth a lot, but that's part of the magic. The treasure chest will know if we don't cross the path at least three times," Rylan explained to Lena.

The duck didn't look convinced.

"You'll see!" Rylan told her and drew one more purple line on the page.

*Meow.*

"Lena, was that you?" Rylan looked at the duck. It didn't make a sound.

The meowing continued.

Rylan got up and tried to find the cat making all the noise.

"Here, kitty, kitty," she called.

A long white tail flicked around the corner of the lake trail. Rylan got up to follow it.

"I'll be right back, Lena," she told the duck.

When Rylan got to the trail, she couldn't see the cat anymore, but she still heard it meowing.

*It must be hurt.* Rylan thought. She didn't know everything about cats, but she knew that they wouldn't cry that much unless something was wrong.

She desperately followed the crying cat around the trail, catching glimpses of it every now and then.

Rylan noticed that she hadn't been on this part of the trail before, but she could still see the lake. She felt confident she could follow the trail back to her tent without a problem. Hopefully, her mom would have a long phone call and not get back before she did.

The trail opened up to a large field housing at least ten different RV's. They were all spread out and the campers were scattered around. Some were playing ball, some were fishing, some were cooking over a fire, and some were reading.

Rylan could see the fluffy white cat clearly now. It was limping towards the closest RV. Rylan continued to follow it.

When she got closer to the vehicle, Rylan heard a woman reading aloud:

*But the angel said to them, "Do not be afraid. I bring you good news that will cause great joy for all the people. Today in the town of David a Savior has been born to you; he is the Messiah, the Lord.*

Rylan knew that story! Lilly read it to her yesterday while they made crafts.

A man's voice read the next verse:
*Suddenly a great company of the heavenly host appeared with the angel, praising God and saying, "Glory to God in the highest heaven, and on earth peace to those on whom his favor rests.*

Rylan couldn't see the cat anymore. She joined the man and woman reading to ask if they knew where the cat went.

"Have you seen a kitty?" Rylan asked them. She continued to gaze around their camping area in hopes of spotting the little white animal.

The woman lifted a blanket in her lap, "Is this the cat you're looking for?"

"Yes!" Rylan squealed and ran over to it.

"This is Billy," the woman told Rylan as she pet the cat.

"I think he has a hurt leg," Rylan informed her.

"I think you're right," the woman agreed. "I'll take him to the vet when we get home."

"What are you doing out here?" The man asked Rylan. He knew she wasn't with the other RV camping groups.

"Celebrating Christmas," Rylan stated and continued petting the cat, Billy.

"That's what we're doing, too!" The woman said.

The man added, "We read the Christmas story every year."

"What is the story?" Rylan remembered Lilly reading about angels and a baby, but the details were fuzzy.

"God's people had been treated badly for a long time. But God promised to send a hero to save them, and he did!" The man explained.

"The hero didn't wear a cape or fight bad guys like people expected. He was a little baby who grew into a man that taught us about peace, love, and forgiveness." The woman smiled at her. "He brought us freedom from sin and gave us eternal life."

"Wow," Rylan was amazed a little baby could do all that. She would ask her mom more about the story later.

Rylan was about to ask the woman more questions about the cat when she heard a familiar banjo coming towards them.

Jamey and Kenaniah came upon the group and immediately stopped playing.

"Rylan!" Jamey exclaimed, "What are you doing out here?"

"You're supposed to be on a treasure hunt back at your campsite," Kenaniah pointed out.

"She went on a different kind of treasure hunt," the woman told them.

"We were just discussing the Christmas story," the man elaborated.

"I followed this kitty," Rylan explained to her church friends. "He was hurt and meowing a lot. I wanted to see if he needed help."

"That's sweet, but we need to get you back to your camp," Jamey said. He could only imagine how upset Emily would be when she realized Rylan was missing.

"Okay, maybe Mom and I can come back later to visit the kitty," Rylan thought aloud.

"That'd be fine with us," the woman assured her.

"Our church is hosting a big candlelight service tonight," Kenaniah reminded everyone, "you can see each other there."

"Rylan!" Ranger Brooks came running up to her. "We've been looking all over for you."

He pulled out his radio and let the others know that Rylan had been found.

# Chapter 13

Emily held Rylan for what seemed like hours. She told the little wanderer over and over again how much she loved her and begged her not to ever leave without permission again.

Rylan felt embarrassed that everyone had been so worried about her. She would definitely avoid any further upset. She was happy to snuggle into her mom, but she was getting bored.

"Is it time for the church service yet?" Rylan asked Emily impatiently. She had a special surprise prepared for her mom during the candlelight service.

"Not yet!" Emily freed Rylan from her embrace. "First, we're going to try a new tradition."

When Ranger Boom received the call that Rylan had been found, Emily insisted that he take her to "campsite 7" immediately. They ate a late lunch with their new RV friends, Greg and Jean.

During lunch, Rylan continued to play with the cat while Emily talked with Jean and Greg about Christmas traditions.

"I always knit Greg and Billy a new set of matching sweaters," Jean giggled.

"Thankfully, Billy usually tears them up. They get uglier every year!" Greg joked. Jean gave his arm a playful shove.

"Who's Billy?" Emily couldn't imagine who would be tearing up a handmade gift year after year.

"The cat," Jean pointed at the fluffy white feline playing on the ground with Rylan.

"Ah," Emily understood now. "That makes more sense."

Greg got them back on topic, "My favorite Christmas tradition is making a birthday card for Jesus."

"Remember the year our cards had a Luau theme?" Jean had been very amused at those cards, "We drew the wise men in hula skirts."

Every year, Jean and Greg made a special birthday card for Jesus. It usually included hand drawn pictures, a heartfelt note, a prayer, and sometimes a bible verse. After the first two years, Jean added in a theme element to the cards to keep the tradition from getting stale. The theme was usually from another culture; Jean enjoyed the culture based themes the most. She knew in her heart that God made all people different and special as part of his amazing creation. He then sent Jesus to save every single one of those people. She saw it as an added element of worship and honor to highlight a different aspect of creation each year.

Emily loved the way Greg and Jean did the birthday cards and wanted to try it with Rylan. Her young artist was bound to enjoy it.

Emily pulled out some paper and crayons for her and Rylan to work with. They drew their favorite memories from the past few days.

Emily's card pictured sunrise over the lake. A heron wandered on one side of the picture, and Lena the wood duck swam at the other end. Emily made a few sprigs of mint grow around the lake. For final touches, she did a soft brown vignette that reminded her of the coffee Jolie shared with her the previous day.

Rylan's card was much different. Emily almost wondered if they had been on the same camping trip.

The little girl drew the waterfall from campsite two, except in her picture it was much taller than in real life. The waterfall spilled into the lake where horses and kittens splashed playfully in the purple waters. Yes, true to her preferences, Rylan colored all the water purple. She added butterflies all over the sky. Emily noticed a sneaky raccoon hiding behind a tree in one corner of the picture.

"Where am I?" Emily felt sad that Rylan hadn't included her in the 'favorite memory' picture.

"This is just the cover!" Rylan assured her. "I ran out of room, so I drew more inside the card."

Emily opened the card up and was happy to see a picture of her and Rylan sitting by the campfire. It was perfect.

Emily wasn't sure how to pick bible verses or write prayers on the cards, but she gave it her best shot.

"Hey, Rylan," Emily began, "do you remember any stories you heard this week that you really liked?"

"Stories? Like how Jean made the Luau card for Christmas one year?"

"Yeah, or how Pastor Ernest talked about joy before we ate hot-dogs," Emily prompted.

Rylan took a moment to earnestly think. "I really liked Lilly reading to me about the angels."

Angels! That was a good starting point. "Why did you like the angel story?" Emily asked.

"Obviously, Angels are super cool," Rylan explained "and they were singing. You know I love singing!"

Emily would ask Her new friends about what scripture would correlate with angels singing.

"What about you, mom?"

Emily wasn't used to anyone asking about her opinions or feelings. She felt proud of her daughter for engaging in conversation but also scared to answer. *What was her favorite story from the week? What if she picked the wrong answer? Could there even be a wrong answer?* This was supposed to be a fun activity. Emily felt stress creeping up on her.

"I'll have to get back to you on that," Emily told Rylan, vowing to herself that she would come up with a good answer.

The sound of hooves plodding on grass and bells ringing filled the clearing. Bliss, Jolie, and Lilly pulled up to Campsite number 1 in the Agape wagon to pick up Emily and Rylan for the Christmas Eve service.

"Hi, Irma! Hi, Louise!" Rylan immediately went to pet the horses.

Emily packed away the coloring supplies they had been using, grabbed an extra blanket, and took her place in the wagon next to Lilly and Rylan.

The group sang "Away in a Manger" on the brief trip to the meeting spot. The horses followed the Lake trail counter clockwise to get there. This was the way Jamey and Kenaniah had come that morning when they visited the RV section.

Irma and Louise came to a gentle stop when they reached the pine stage. The ladies hopped out of the wagon, gave the horses a treat and some water, then filtered into one of the wooden benches. The stage was backed by Agape Lake, so the seated audience had a lovely view.

Emily was excited to see what would take place during the service. Jamey was entertaining the early arrivals with a soft strumming of "Little Drummer Boy" while the rangers unpacked small white vigil candles and fire blankets.

Jean and Greg arrived and sat behind Rylan. She was disappointed to learn that Billy the cat wasn't with them.

"Santa needed his help tonight," Greg explained to the disappointed little girl.

"Billy works for Santa?" Rylan didn't know what use Santa might have for a cat on Christmas Eve.

"Actually, he is Santa's most valued employee," Jean told her.

"What's his job?" Rylan imagined the cat pulling the sleigh with Rudolph.

"He distracts anyone who might be awake from seeing Santa."

"How?"

"By meowing, of course!"

"That's a good job for him," Rylan said. "He is a very distracting meower."

Ethel, Ruthie, Edwin, and Eden sat down in the front row. Edwin and Eden had a mysterious box with them and a bright red thermos.

DJ and Isaiah sat on the row behind them with several family members. The church group filled up most of the seating.

Emily noticed the park manager, Pam, sitting on the back row. She had at least four other people gathered near her. Were they related to Ranger Brooks, too? Emily hoped she would get a chance to meet everyone before the trip was over. Camping brought out her social side.

The rangers finished lighting candles all over the stage and took a seat near the front. Pastor Ernest walked to the center of the stage and the service began.

"Friends and family," he shouted out into the night, "I would like to wish you a very merry Christmas. Please bow your heads with me as we pray over this service."

Everyone took a moment to close their eyes and clear their mind. Ernest prayed, "We thank you, Father God for sending your son to earth; for letting him be a perfect example and sacrifice for us. Tonight we honor the miracles and blessings you have bestowed. We praise you, Father. We want to spread the good news of your love. We pray that you stop the plans of the enemy over those who don't know you yet. We beseech that your light will fill all corners of the earth, letting the whole world feel your goodness. God, we pray that tonight we feel the same celebration that was felt that first Christmas. Let us feel the joy that can only come from knowing that our savior lives. Amen."

"Amen," the crowd resounded.

"I'll now ask that sister Linda starts off our celebration with a birthday song," Ernest exited the stage and Linda, one of the ladies who spoke to Rylan about decorating her room, moved to the front.

Linda sang "Happy Birthday, Jesus" and "Do You Hear What I Hear?" Emily was delighted to see that Rylan sang along in a few places.

After Linda's songs, Ranger Brooks sang "Christmas Shoes" and "Mary, Did You Know?" Those had the whole audience in tears.

The soloists finished with Jolie performing "Breath of Heaven." After that, the congregation was invited to sing traditional carols as a group and to light their candles.

The group singing started off with "Silent Night." Ranger Brooks and Ranger Boom lit their candles and went down opposite ends of the pews to light the others.

"Need a flame?" Ranger Brooks leaned close to Emily and lit her candle with his own.

She had a difficult time remembering the words to the song as she lit Rylan's candle.

Before the gathering concluded with "Joy to the World," Ernest returned to the stage. The night stars were ablaze behind him. The lake reflected the light of the stars and the candles in a scene that was like heaven on earth.

"It has been a truly holy and special night," the pastor announced. "But this trip has been a unique blessing in other ways, as well." He motioned for someone to come forward.

To Emily's surprise, Lilly and Rylan stood up and walked towards the front on the stage.

Ernest continued, "Our group had the honor of meeting many new faces this year. One of those new faces was this young one right here," he placed his hand on Rylan's shoulder. "She has a song she'd like to share with you."

Ernest stepped back. Lilly began to hum and gave Rylan an encouraging smile.

*Twinkle twinkle Christmas Star*
*In our hearts is where you are*
*Leading us to love and sing*
*Spreading joy and spreading peace*

*Twinkle twinkle Christmas star*
*Shine on all near and far*
*Thank you for your many gifts*
*Blessings blessings Aaa-aaa-mennn*

Emily applauded harder than she ever had before. Watching Rylan sing was the best gift she could have ever received, or so she thought.

Rylan and Lilly returned to their seats and everyone began "Joy to the World." Unfortunately, they did not make it very far.

As soon as the group had cheerfully belted out "the Lord has come," a very angry man burst into the clearing.

"That's right the Lord has come!" He screamed. "The wrath of the Lord!"

Emily heard two gasps and an "Oh no," come from the pew behind her.

The angry man continued shouting, "Who broke my window? You best come forth!"

DJ and Isaiah began to stand up to face 'Old Jed's Wrath,' but before they could, one of the men in the front row did.

"Jed! So glad you could join us," Edwin said.

"We have a brand new window for you here in this box," Eden held the box out to him.

Skeptical, the old man opened the box.

"Skunk!" He shouted and dropped the box. The poor skunk lazily crawled out and looked at the frightened man. Edwin pulled out some treats and the skunk turned.

"No, no, not that end," Jed backed away. "We'll settle this tomorrow!" He warned and then disappeared back into the night.

"Excellent work, Romeo," Eden told the skunk as Edwin scooped it back up.

"I told you they were horrid pranksters," Ethel said to Ruthie.

"All things work together for good," Ruthie shrugged.

The skunk was harmless. It had been a family pet for years. Edwin and Eden loved to scare people with it, especially at large gatherings.

Before Ernest returned to the stage, Ethel offered him the red thermos the boys had been carrying.

"Here's a special Christmas drink for you, pastor. We so appreciate you," Ethel said as she handed off the thermos.

"Thank you, ma'am! I was getting thirsty," Ernest took several gulps of the drink. It was some sort of hot chocolate concoction.

He returned to the stage. "Jesus brought us hope, forgiveness, compassion, and love. A broken world in need of love received it. The prince of peace is here. He is calling to all of us to follow him. He's not dead! Jesus is alive. You can be alive, too. This Christmas, don't hesitate to celebrate and share the good news." With that, he restarted "Joy to the World."

When the song was over, Ernest tried to preach some more, but after several yawns he gave up. "Well, folks, I guess all that rejoicing took a toll on this old pastor. I need to get off to bed," he was asleep before he was able to sit back down.

"Ernest!" Lilly jumped up and ran to her husband. She had seen a lot of bizarre behavior out of him over the years, but never this.

"Don't worry, sugar!" Ethel told her cheerily. "My special Christmas drink makes everyone do that."

"What is it?" Lilly was still full of concern.

"Warm milk, chocolate powder, vanilla extract, cinnamon, and one of Ruthie's sedatives."

"Ethel!" Ruthie exclaimed, "No wonder the boys turned out so bad."

"I just thought we could all use an early night," Ethel defended herself. "I want to be well rested for Christmas Day."

And well rested they were. Everyone spent a happy night sleeping under the stars, imagining angels singing.

Before the gathering went their separate ways, Emily got Ranger Boom's attention.

"Do you know any good bible verses about angels?" She asked him. She needed it for Rylan's Christmas card.

Nate was glad to see Emily had opened her mind up to bible study. "Try Luke 15:10," he said and gave her the Bible out of his pocket.

Emily started to open the book, but Nate stopped her. "You can keep that bible," he said. "I have plenty of others. You might like reading all of Luke tomorrow. Right now we need to get everyone back to their campsites."

# Chapter 14

*December 25, 2020*

Merry Christmas! Emily felt abuzz with new life. She felt giddy. The real spirit of Christmas had entered her heart for the first time since she was an adolescent.

Rylan was still sleeping. Yesterday was long, but ended well. Emily worked on her birthday card for Jesus while she waited on Rylan to wake naturally.

Well, she tried to work on the card. Emily stared at the blank inner page. What bible verse was meaningful to her? What prayer did she want to pray?

She pulled out the bible Nate gave to her the previous night and tried to turn to Luke as he suggested. She went too far and found herself in the book of Acts. The words about seeking God jumped right off the page at her.

*"God, who made the world and everything in it, is Lord of heaven and earth. He doesn't live in temples made with human hands. Nor is God served by human hands, as though he needed something, since he is the one who gives life, breath, and everything else. From one person God created every human nation to live on the whole earth, having determined their appointed times and the boundaries of their lands. God made the nations so they would seek him, perhaps even reach out to him and find him. In fact, God isn't far away from any of us. In God we live, move, and exist. As some of your own poets said, 'We are his offspring.' "Therefore, as God's offspring, we have no need to imagine that the divine being is like a gold, silver, or stone image made by human skill and thought. God overlooks ignorance of these things in*

*times past, but now directs everyone everywhere to change their hearts and lives."*
*Acts of the Apostles 17:24-30 CEB*

For the first time, Emily felt like she might have something in common with God. She, too, wanted to be sought out. She resolved right then to start pursuing God the way she wanted to be pursued, and the way he was already pursuing her. She turned back to the Old Testament and continued reading. One of the first ways you get to know any person is by asking about their past. The Old Testament is definitely the past. Emily had a hard time fathoming just how old the beginning of time is.

"Getting to know God might take some time," She said aloud, completing her realization that the Lord and creator of everything she knew was waiting on her to get to know him. She saw learning in a new way. She wished she could relive her school years and look at things through a "God Lense."

She began to write everything "God is" on her notes page. She knew that she would never be able to capture everything that God is, but she trusted that the qualities he wanted to be revealed to her would manifest.

"Boo!" Rylan jumped out at Emily from behind the log on which she was studying on.

"Wrong holiday!" Emily joked. "Merry Christmas," she gave Rylan a big hug.

"Merry Christmas!" Rylan returned the greeting and hug. "Where's breakfast?"

She must be having a growth spurt. "We have to find breakfast," Emily informed her.

Rylan didn't look pleased. "Are we eating pine cones or something?"

"Nope!" Emily stood and packed the Bible up in her bag along with the card supplies from yesterday. "Grab your treasure map."

"Finally!" Rylan lit up with joy, she had been waiting all week for the treasure hunt.

The pair set off down the Agape Lake Trail in search of buried treasure. Rylan was not aware of the actual location or contents of the treasure, and Emily was not aware of the many intricacies built into Rylan's map.

"Stop!" Rylan shrieked. They hadn't gone far. Emily could still see their tent.

"Forget something?" Emily asked.

"No, we have to turn around and ask someone for directions." Rylan informed her.

"Okay," Emily looked around. "Who are we asking?"

"Maybe that tree?" Rylan pointed to the first tree at the trailhead.

"That tree looks full of itself," Emily observed. "The second one would probably be friendlier."

"Good point!" Rylan ran down the trail to the tree, knocked, listened, and returned triumphantly.

"The tree says we have to collect something pretty and give it to the pine cone over there. Then the pine cone will tell you the next clue."

"And what does your map say?"

"The map says after we talked to the trees, we play tag three times, roll over once, and do a special handshake. Then the treasure will appear."

Emily followed her directions. After the handshake, Emily excitedly pointed at a fresh mound of dirt by a tree on the left.

"That looks like a treasure spot to me!" Emily said.

Rylan looked genuinely surprised. She intended to make up a pretend treasure when they finished her "map".

"Let's go dig it up," Emily urged.

Jamey and Kenaniah hadn't buried the treat bag too deep. Each girl only had to scoop off three layers of dirt.

Emily pulled out the bag and asked Rylan if they should open it.

"Yes!" Rylan was bursting with anticipation.

Inside the bag were two bottles of water, two cinnamon rolls, one banana, one apple, and one star.

The star was made of sticks tied together and painted with glitter.

"That's what I made with Lilly the night you went to look for the cooler," Rylan explained. "But I don't know how it got here."

"I guess it is a Christmas miracle!" Emily was feeling very emotional. She loved the star.

"I thought it could be our special star this year since we didn't bring ours," Rylan looked around them.

"What are you looking for?"

"A tree short enough for you to put the star on."

Emily knew they wouldn't find that.

"What about a tree short enough for you to put the star on? I can hold you up."

They found a reachable treetop and adorned it. It might have been a tree limb instead of a top, but it worked just as well. They settled in for breakfast and finished making Jesus' birthday cards. Emily knew what to write now.

In Rylan's card, she inscribed the 'angel' verse and helped Rylan come up with a prayer.

*In the same way, I tell you, joy breaks out in the presence of God's angels over one sinner who changes both heart and life.*
Luke 15:10 CEB

The prayer went:
*Happy birthday, Jesus! I hope you and the angels are having a good Christmas. Thank you for us finding the treasure and getting good directions from the tree and pine cone. I love you.*
-Rylan

Emily's verse was:

*When Jesus came to that spot, he looked up and said, " Zacchaeus, come down at once. I must stay in your home today."*
Luke 19:5 CEB

She felt very much like Zacchaeus that day. She was searching for God, trying to see him, and almost climbed a tree. She was thankful that Jesus was alive and with them in spirit. It wouldn't have been much of a celebration without the birthday boy. Jesus would be staying in her home every day.

Emily wasn't able to write her prayer until later. Rylan wanted to sing and go visit some of her friends around the camp. She tucked the Christmas cards into her new-used bible and dedicated herself to the festivities.

When Rylan and Emily joined the church camper, Emily was surprised to see her friend Emory speaking to the group.

Bliss waved the newcomers over.

"What's going on?" Emily whispered.

"Emory is sharing a devotional about bitterness," Bliss whispered back. "She just started by reading a bible verse from Hebrews."

*That's an odd choice for Christmas Day*, Emily thought.

"On Christmas Day two years ago," Emory addressed her little audience, "I finally began the process of healing my wounds. I thought forgiving any past hurts was enough. I didn't realize that I had to replant myself in good soil to fully get the bitterness out of my roots."

Emory paused for a little bit longer than she should have, Emily thought she might be getting nervous. Her heart went out to the young woman. Public speaking was no easy task, especially when sharing something so personal.

Emory took a deep breath, "I wrote letters of apology to anyone that I thought might have something against me. I was worried about their responses, so I went off-grid. I took down all social media. I was soon surprised at how many letters I received in response to the ones I sent."

Emily realized that the earlier conversation she'd had with Emory about letter writing stemmed from a much different place than she thought.

The young woman continued, "I was immediately relieved when I started to receive kind letter responses. I gained many pen pals from the experience. I started living with only the bare minimum and traveling a lot. These verses are the ones that helped me on my journey."

Emory read off the following scriptures:

Matthew 5:24
Leave your gift at the altar until you make peace with all who are angry with you.

James 5:16
If you have sinned, you should tell each other what you have done. Then you can pray for one another and be healed.

Colossians 3:15
Each one of you is part of the body of Christ, and you were chosen to live together in peace. Let the peace of Christ control your

thoughts and be grateful.

After she read Colossians 3:15, she shyly sat down. Pastor Long hopped up and raised his hands high.

"I love to hear a testimony!" He shouted. "Thank you, sister Emory, for sharing your experience. I now pray to our heavenly Father to eradicate any roots of bitterness in our lives and to give us the courage to turn to You only for every good and perfect thing. Lord, you know that bitterness creeps in when we expect good things from broken people. We beg for compassion, peace, patience, wisdom and understanding in our dealings with others. In Jesus' name, Amen."

Emily was stunned at how relevant the message was for her own personal problems. Just a few days ago she was thinking about bitterness and how it was taking a toll on her and, consequently, Rylan. She'd be meditating on the things she learned that day.

Emily found Emory after the meeting adjourned and told her what a great job she did.

"Really?" Emory blushed deeply. "I'm never sure if I'm saying the right thing," she admitted.

"I feel that way almost all the time," Emily agreed.

Lilly overheard the girls talking and couldn't help but interject, "I find that when you share out of love, the fear falls away."

Lilly knew she shared that particular nugget of wisdom often, but she didn't care. It was shared out of love.

That evening, Jamey and Kenaniah performed their new song, "Guide Me."

*Where I need to be*
*Where I need to go*
*Where I've already been*
*Only God knows*

*The B.I.B.L.E*
*It is leadin me*
*Following that Roman Road*
*to the sanctuary*

*God will you guide me*
*God will you hide me*
*From this world filled with sin*
*I only want your love in*

*All my carefully laid plans*
*Crumble into sand*
*When the lord of the earth*
*Says to put him first*

*Will you guide me*
*(Will you hide me)*
*Will you find me*
*(Will you guide me)*

*Keep on Wandering aimlessly*
*Watching others run and flee*
*Im just trying to be free*
*Will you guide me*

*Open arms await me*
*My path he will make straight*
*Rejoice and celebrate*
*God will guide me*

## Chapter 15

*December 26, 2020*

Ranger Brooks chased after Emily as she walked to her car.

"Wait," he called to her, "I almost forgot your Christmas gift."

Emily was delighted that the ranger seemed to care so much. She took the carefully wrapped box from him, wondering if it were something from his herb garden

"It's a phone number," Emily frowned as she pulled a scrap of notebook paper out of the box with ten digits scribbled on it.

"My phone number," Gabe beamed.

Emily decided to accept the gesture as cute. "I suppose I'll be talking to you soon."

"I hope so," he replied. "I'd like to know if you find your cooler."

Emily gave him a nod and started to get in her car.

Gabe stopped her again. "There's actually one more thing under the tissue paper."

"What, your address?" Emily quipped.

"No, I didn't think you needed that. I live here."

Emily lifted the tissue paper that had been resting under the ranger's phone number. There, at the bottom of the box, was some dirt.

Emily raised an eyebrow at Gabe.

"I planted some mint for you," Gabe explained. "I know you said you don't have a green thumb, but mint is easy. Just don't forget to water it."

Emily decided her earlier thought was right, the gift was cute.

As they drove away from Agape Poppy, Emily was already planning their return trip. She couldn't wait to get back.

"Mom?" Rylan interrupted Emily's pensive mood.

"Yes, dear?"

"Can we go ice skating today?"

Unbelievable! On the way home from camping, this kid wanted to stop for some quick skating. Emily thought it was a good thing she was well rested that day.

"Sure! I don't have a good reason not to," Emily knew of an ice skating place near a car dealership on their way back to town.

When they arrived, Emily felt disappointed at all the people. She wished she could be free to skate around as fast as she wanted and to try doing some tricks, but that would look silly for a grown woman. Instead, she contented herself with holding Rylan's hand as they slowly slid around the arena.

After the third time around, Emily convinced Rylan to let go of the bar and do some twirls with her. At least if Rylan was twirling with Emily it wouldn't look silly.

Emily almost told Rylan how lucky she was to have such a fun mom, but then decided better.

"Rylan?"

"Yeah, Mom?"

"I'm lucky to have a kid as fun as you."

*"Those who control their tongue will have a long life; opening your*

*mouth can ruin everything." Proverbs 13:3*

On the way out of the ice skating arena, Emily and Rylan saw a disheveled man standing on the sidewalk. He held a sign that read "anything helps."

"Why is that man standing there?" Rylan asked her mom with concern in her sweet brown eyes.

"He wants money," Emily replied and tried to rush her daughter into the car.

"Why does he want money?" Rylan wasn't dropping the subject.

"I don't know," Emily answered honestly. She didn't know anything about that man.

"Maybe he'd like a Christmas star." Rylan offered.

"He probably doesn't have one," Emily agreed.

"I have one," Rylan said.

"I don't want to give away the special one you made me," Emily told her, eager to get going. They were both buckled in now and Emily was ready to back out.

"What about this one?" Rylan pulled out Grandma Mildred's special tin star from a bag in the floorboard.

Emily was shocked.

"How did Grandma's star get here?"

"I brought it just in case we needed it," Rylan admitted.

Emily looked at the star hard and all of the lessons she had learned over the past week flooded over her into one feeling: love.

Emily gently lifted the sweet potato stained tag, "God will guide you."

"Okay, we can give him the star." Emily smiled at Rylan and felt thankful for the opportunity to share God's love. The love that shone so brightly through her daughter and that she hoped would begin to shine brightly in her as well.

Emily pulled the tag off and quickly made a new one that said the same thing. The man could have the star, but she wasn't ready to part with that particular tag.

She helped Rylan get back out of the car and they walked over to the man.

"We thought you'd like a special Christmas star," Rylan said as she handed him the tin tree topper.

The man looked hard at the star. He seemed to hate it and love it all at the same time.

After a pause longer than Emily was comfortable with, he took it from Rylan's outstretched hand and grumbled "thanks."

He turned the handcrafted item over and checked the initials etched into the back.

"A Chip Rangley star," he said in a voice more wealthy sounding than Emily expected.

How did everyone know about this Chip Rangley? Except for being informed about his fame at the airport last year, Emily had still never heard of him.

"So I've heard," Emily replied. "Have a happy new year."

She nudged Rylan back towards the car.

"I might." He said and continued to stare at the star.

Once they were back on the road, Rylan brought up a tense subject.

"Do you think my other mom is outside like that man was?"

Rylan almost never brought up her birth mother. Aside from nine months incubating, she had never met the woman, and the only reason she was aware of her existence is because of the prodding questions that had been asked about the absence of a father.

Emily did know Rylan's father. She loved him. He was her reason for getting up most days before the days grew too twisted to fight for. He loved her, too, but he was too broken to love her right. Emily knew now that God could have fixed him, could have fixed them both, but they weren't pursuing God at the time.

Instead, they were pursuing themselves. The problem with pursuing yourself is that you aren't perfect. Chasing imperfection while expecting to find something good leads to bitter disappointment. Rylan's father knew that all too well. He passed away from his overwhelming disappointment before he even found out about Rylan. Rylan's mother was one of the women he had been chasing in that pursuit of self.

When Emily found out the woman didn't want to keep the baby, she volunteered to adopt her without a second thought. Rylan is exactly what Emily always wanted.

"I don't think so, sweet heart." Emily was alarmed at Rylan's concern and wasn't sure how to discuss the other mother. "I'll see if I can check on her when we get home."

"That sounds good," Rylan didn't like talking about it either, but, like all children, she couldn't help but love her mother.

*"Love is patient, love is kind. It does not envy, it does not boast, it is not proud. It does not dishonor others, it is not self-seeking, it is not easily angered, it keeps no record of wrongs. Love does not delight in evil but rejoices with the truth. It always protects, always trusts, always hopes, always perseveres. Love never fails."*
*1 Corinthians 13:4-8*

# Chapter 16

Emily was stricken with anxiety when they got home. Her renter taped a note to the fridge reading "CALL ASAP!!!" She did just that.

"Hello?" A cheerful and musical female voice answered.

"Hi, Mrs. Lacey. This is Emily. I just got home and read your note, is everything okay?"

"It will be if you agree to be my new manager," Mrs. Lacey replied lightly.

"Manager of what?" Emily definitely did not understand.

"My new restaurant, Sunny Sage." She stated matter of factly. "I already have a gardener and a chef. But I need someone with administrative experience, good customer service, and a penchant for flavor. After sampling the contents of your cooler, I believe you are my manager."

Emily and Mrs. Lacey met four years ago through work. Mrs. Lacey is the chair of the Southeastern Holistic Medicine Consortium (SHMC). Emily oversaw a grant project gifted to her employer by the SHMC. By working on this project together, she and Mrs. Lacey became fast friends despite the age gap.

Mrs. Lacey is the usual tenant at Emily's condo when she takes her annual Christmas vacation. Mrs. Lacey has family in Cedartown that she likes to visit at that time of year, but she is a devoted resident of North Carolina.

Managing Sunny Sage sounded like a dream job. Emily couldn't believe that leaving the cooler behind had resulted in such an opportunity. She was up for a promotion at her current place of work, though. The decision would be a difficult one.

Before she hung up, Mrs. Lacey got a tone of mischief in her voice. "Have you spoken to Janet since returning from your trip?"

Emily was surprised at the question, "No, I just got in and called you ASAP like your note said."

"Good," Mrs. Lacey said smugly. "I'm glad to see you take me seriously! I wish more people did. You might want to give Janet a call. I think I'll be talking to you again very soon."

Emily had a small idea what the cryptic message could be. One of the grants she frantically applied for a few weeks ago was with Mrs. Lacey's Consortium, the SHMC.

Emily decided she'd better call Janet right away.

"You did it!" Janet beamed over the phone. "You got the SHMC grant! Our office is saved for at least another year and your position is fully funded."

Emily felt a wave of relief wash over her. Now her old job was saved and she had a new opportunity.

The new project was to evaluate effective remedies for COVID symptoms in a pediatric setting from a holistic approach. They would be meeting first thing after the holiday break to work out the details.

# Chapter 17

February 1st, 2021

Emily's phone was ringing nonstop again. She was dropping papers trying to answer it, an all too familiar scene.

"Yes, Janet, I did submit the invoice." Emily assured her longtime boss, friend, and mentor at Caring for Kids.

When faced with the decision on whether to change careers or not, Emily couldn't bring herself to part with her beloved non-profit.

However, she also wasn't going to pass up the opportunity to work towards her dream.

She had come to a compromise. Emily was now working remotely for the nonprofit and spent most of her business hours managing Sunny Sage. It was a fun and busy time, and she was learning a lot.

Emily and Rylan began attending church at Shepherd Springs with their friends from Agape Poppy and devoted Sundays to family time.

Emily wore a bright blue apron with yellow trim that Lilly made especially for her new role at Sunny Sage. She flipped the restaurant sign to 'Open' and made sure everything was presentable for the day's patrons.

The door bell tingled and she launched into her usual, "Welcome to Sunny Sage!" Before she saw who it was.

Ranger Brooks stood before her, smiling as big as he possibly could.

"You never called," he observed. She was still as beautiful as he remembered.

"No, I wanted to, but I've had a lot to do with the business," she trailed off. It was true, she had thought of him often and had thought of calling. But she hated talking on the phone, especially to people she hardly knew. She figured that if he wanted to talk to her badly enough he would find her, and he did.

"That's okay," Gabe shrugged. He had been busy, too. The night Emily left the campground his dad showed up. His dad who supposedly died ten years ago. Gabe decided he'd better not unload all of that on her right away.

"I like your restaurant," He noticed many traces of his campgrounds in her decor choices.

"Well, it's not technically mine, but there's a season for everything," she trailed off. "Would you like to try the tea of the day?"

"What kind is it?" He asked, ignoring the specials board.

"Mint."

They shared a smile and he was happy to see a twinkle in her eye that hadn't been there before.

"I won't say no to a favorite," he grinned. "Let me grab my...friend out of the car. I'll be right back."

Gabe hadn't been sure if the visit with Emily would be a long one or not, so he had left his recently resurrected father in the car.

Emily poured three cups of tea and was ready at a table when the men got back in.

Gabe sat down next to her, but his friend stayed behind in the doorway.

"What's wrong?" Gabe called to him.

"It's the star girl," the man replied, looking embarrassed.

"Now that is a small world," Gabe looked at Emily. "You saved him."

Emily was very confused. *Was this the man she and Rylan had given Grandma's special star to?*

The man walked over and shook Emily's hand from across the table.

"I'm Chip Rangley."

Emily was stunned.

"Emily O'Dell," she automatically replied.

"His name is really Jacob Brooks." Gabe explained, "He's my father."

Emily soon learned that Jacob Brooks became an alcoholic after his cancer diagnosis in 2005. Ashamed of what he had become, he fled from his family and changed his name to Chip Rangley. He supported himself by making art out of the only thing he could afford: trash. Some of his best sellers early on where tin star tree toppers. By some miracle, the media decided he was a green hero for working with recycled materials and made his work an expensive trend. He enjoyed the success for a few years, but the joy wasn't genuine and didn't last. He still struggled with alcoholism and felt worthless and ashamed. He longed to make things right with his family and was trying to work up the nerve to do that on the night Emily and Rylan found him. Seeing his old star with the gift tag was the nudge he needed to go home.

"It's nice to meet you," Emily gave Jacob's hand another shake after hearing his story. She wondered if this was part of why Pam had the dream about the house falling down. She also wondered how much Pam knew about this.

"You too," Jacob said, visibly relieved to have his story told.

Other customers started coming into the quaint cafe.

"I guess you need to get back to work," Gabe nodded towards the newcomers.

"Looks like it," Emily agreed. "I'll call this time," she promised.

"I'm counting on it."

The men finished their teas and then made their way back to the car.

"A ticket!" Gabe complained.

Apparently that was a no parking zone.

"Too bad they didn't put a boot on your wheel," Jacob joked. "I could have made a pretty nice sculpture out of that."

*"Therefore, if anyone is in Christ, the new creation has come: The old has gone, the new is here!"*
*2 Corinthians 5:17*

## Preview

## Agape Poppy Campground Adventures Book 2: Resurrected Dreams, An Easter Story

*"The truly happy person doesn't follow wicked advice, doesn't stand on the road of sinners, and doesn't sit with the disrespectful."*
*Psalms 1:1*

Bliss read the invitation from William with mounting shock.

You are invited to celebrate the union of Miss Bliss Ogle and Mister William Baker on Sunday, April 4th, 2021 at Sunset by the Agape Poppy Waterfall. No gifts, please.

When she finished reading, Lilly snatched the invite from her to read it again.

"Did you know about this?" Ranger Brooks asked Bliss.

Ranger Gabriel Brooks was one of two permanent rangers who managed the campground year round. Most of the regular campers called him Gabe. His mother, Pam Brooks, was the owner of the campground.

"I dreamed about it, but I never imagined it would really happen," Bliss told him. She stood there smiling, unsure of what to do.

Relieved that Bliss seemed happy at the unexpected news, Gabe proceeded with his Ranger duties:

"Since William isn't here, I'll need you to come down to the ranger station with me to fill out the event paperwork. We might be easy going here, but the paperwork still has to be in order."

"Paperwork!" Lilly exclaimed. "We have to find a dress and a cake!" She couldn't believe this man was concerned about paperwork when her best friend's wedding was in two days.

Gabe was hoping for this reaction, he loved to get people stirred up. He really had another reason for wanting the women to come to the station.

*Find out what happens at the Easter Wedding when a surprise visitor comes to visit! Resurrected Dreams will be finished in March 2022.*

Made in United States
Orlando, FL
30 November 2022